O C E A N

B E A U F O R T

KUPARUK COAST

Oliktok R.

Colville R.

Kuparuk R.

Umiat

R   A   N   G   E

HERSCHEL I.

CAPE HERSCHEL

Firth R.

UNITED STATES

CANADA

| 0 | | 50 | | 100 Miles |

| 0 | 50 | 100 | | 150 Kilometers |

Akiviak

A NOVEL BASED ON THE LIFE
OF A FRONTIER ESKIMO

Kaare Rodahl

W · W · NORTON & COMPANY   New York

FIRST AMERICAN EDITION

Library of Congress Cataloging in Publication Data

Rodahl, Kaare, 1917–
Akiviak : a novel based on the life
of a frontier Eskimo.

1.Eskimos—Alaska—Fiction.   I.Title.
PZ3.R6103   1979   [PT8951.28.022]   839.8'2'374
ISBN 0-393-01181-X   78-24502

Book design by A. Clark Goodman
Display type is typositor York and American Uncial
Text type is C.R.T. Avanta
Manufactured by The Haddon Craftsmen.
1 2 3 4 5 6 7 8 9 0

TO JOAN

who was with me
all the way

PUBLISHER'S NOTE

THE author, who is a physician and a physiologist, spent several years in Northern Alaska together with his wife, studying the physiology of the Eskimos, their nutrition, and acclimatization to cold. They lived among them. He occasionally served as their doctor, and thus gained an intimate knowledge of these people, their way of life, and the country in which they lived, hunted, and traveled.

The purpose of their stay was to discover why the Eskimos get along better in the Arctic than the white man. The author found that the answer is simply that the Eskimo has adjusted himself completely, both physically and mentally, to Arctic conditions.

One day in 1950, in the course of these studies on the north coast of Alaska, the author met the Stone-Age Akiviak. A full-blooded Eskimo, he had been born on the tundra long before any contact with the white man, at a time when his tribe, the nomadic caribou hunters, kindled their fire with flint and lived by their bows and arrows. They soon became friends, and Akiviak gradually revealed his life story to the author, who, with the knowledge he had gained through his research, realized that he had a unique opportunity to combine all this into a book. However, because of other commitments, it was not until 1973 that this could materialize. It was originally written in the author's native language, Norwegian. The present book is an English translation by the author.

This, then, is Akiviak's story, the story of a man who in the span of a lifetime experienced the whole transition from Stone Age to Atomic Age. We follow him, step by step, through famine and feast, sorrow and joy, through conflicts and successes. In spite of the drastic changes that occurred in implements, weapons, methods, and the way of life, the man himself remained the same all the way.

CONTENTS

Akiviak

1

OUT OF THE FOG

HE appeared out of the fog, walking down the slope from the mountains. When the sun broke through the mist behind him, it looked as if he was pushing his own shadow across the tundra.

This was Akiviak, the man who had made the journey from Stone Age to Atomic Age in the span of a lifetime.

"Welcome," he said as he came, and smiled. His look was intensely strong, as if generations of accumulated will were concentrated in this one mind. He looked beyond me, as if staring at a distant object. In the reflections in his dark eyes I saw that it was the airplane behind me that he was focusing on; the airplane that had brought me there.

He was leaning forward as if bending against the wind, even though it was calm. He was small of stature, lean, but muscular and very agile. His skin was tanned. He had no beard. His hair, so black that it was almost blue, covered his forehead. He was dressed in fur, but his trousers were made of blue gaberdine. A camera hung from a string of sinew around his neck.

I wanted to take his picture, but he protested. "No, not my picture. I have always been here; I would rather take a picture of you, a newcomer."

He tried to adjust his camera, but was unable to see properly because of the strong glare from the snow.

"I need my goggles," he said, and started to search for something in the bag he carried over his shoulder. He failed to find what he sought, then he looked as if something had suddenly occurred to him, and he said, "Oh, I forgot. I don't have them anymore."

When he realized that I did not understand what he was talking about, he looked embarrassed and explained that sungoggles were something he had worn to avoid snow blindness. It was simply a piece of wood tied in front of the eyes, with two slots in it, one in front of each eye.

He then put on his spectacles and took a picture. When this was done he led me into his house, a shack on the brink by the Arctic Ocean. A radio antenna swayed between two poles on the roof.

We went through a door of weather-bleached driftwood and came into a hallway. Fur clothing hung from the roof; chunks of frozen caribou meat lay on the floor. In a corner rattled an electric generator. The rest was mostly rubbish, pots and pans, firewood, a tub filled with urine. We opened a door with a wooden lock and came into the main room. The walls were covered with biblical pictures and pages from a mail-order catalogue. A single electric bulb was swinging from the ceiling, and glimmered with power from the generator in the hallway. On the floor sat the children, the smaller ones in a circle around a tin plate filled with caribou meat. They raised their eyes, pushed back their parka hoods and licked their fingers. In a corner another group of youngsters stood close by a radio set, listening so intensely that they paid no attention to us.

Suddenly a roar came from the radio, with such volume that the loudspeaker rattled; it drowned out the voice of the announcer. I soon gathered that what we had heard was the first test blast of the hydrogen bomb in the Pacific, an explosion so tremendous that it wiped out everything within a radius of several miles, and generated heat equivalent to several million degrees.

"The Atomic Age has indeed begun," declared the voice of the announcer.

"What a miracle!" Those were Akiviak's words. He was standing there with his mouth open.

"Can it be done? Is it possible to generate so much heat?"

He had a front tooth which was loose. It vibrated back and forth every time he took a breath. He made an abrupt motion, as if he suddenly had an idea. Excitedly, he threw out his arms:

"Imagine if we had such a bomb here. Then we could melt all the ice so that the ocean would be open all the year."

He turned to the window and looked at his motorboat, which was turned upside down and propped up against a huge slab of ice on the beach. There came a grinding sound from the shore ice under the pressure of the rising tide. As if to himself, he said quietly:

"I would never have thought that I should live to see this happen in my time here on earth."

I could not refrain from asking:

"Was it not better the way it was?"

"Perhaps it was," he replied, nodding thoughtfully, and repeated the statement in his own native tongue: *"Nara."* Then he added, as if by way of an afterthought:

"But we were heathens then."

He brought out his handkerchief and polished his glasses, took his bible and went into the schoolhouse next door, where his little congregation sat assembled on benches along the wall. Akiviak seated himself in a chair under the lamp and called to his son-in-law, Putu. Putu moved silently like a cat in his soft sealskin mukluks, slid into a chair by the table, and opened his bible. The text was from St. Matthew, Chapter 19. Akiviak asked Nuna to read. The pretty little girl bent over the book, her hair falling forward, covering the pages. She stroked it to the side and began reading, her finger pointing to each word as she progressed. She spelled out the text word for word and struggled along until she came to the end. Then Akiviak stood up and explained:

"A rich man came to the Lord seeking to be saved. And the Lord said unto him: 'Sell your property and share your wealth with the poor. Then come and follow me.' But the rich man went away, sorrowful."

Akiviak sat down. A large tray of caribou meat was brought in. He took the tray and said:

"Take this and share it."

When they had shared the meat, they all went home. I could hear the crunch of frozen snow under their mukluks as they walked.

Akiviak and I were alone. The electric light had been put out —they had to stop the generator to save fuel. Instead they burned blubber in a stone lamp; it shed a dim light around the table. We remained silent for a while. Finally I asked, in order to get him started:

"Did you not come from the Utukok River, Akiviak?"

He answered this negative question with a denial, as was the custom, and said No, meaning that he did. The question had aroused his interest. He looked up and asked: "Have you seen it?"

I explained that I had flown along the river all the way from the watershed, where it starts as a stream, until it floods into the sea at Icy Cape.

"But I have paddled it in a skin boat in both directions many a time," he said with a smile.

He was facing me without really looking at me. His unwrinkled skin and colorful complexion were almost ageless in the flickering light of the blubber lamp. There was a distant look in his eyes, as if he were thinking back.

II

THE BEGINNING

He began his life in a tent on the tundra, drifting with the river to the coast in the spring with the rest of his tribe. From his mother he had heard that he had a sister who died the year he was born. Thus, according to their belief, he inherited her soul in addition to his own. In this way he got two souls and became twice as clever as the others, for in addition to being a man, he was given a woman's instincts. He became two persons in one body, yet he was only one human being. He was given the name Akiviak and thereby inherited the name-soul of his great grandfather, a famous hunter who eventually became a shaman. According to legend, he ended his life in the mountains doing battle with the evil spirits, the Kivitoks.

Among his first recollections was the journey back into the mountains: a convoy of skin boats, or umiaks, up the Utukok River on a late summer's day. The Utukok raged between gentle slopes that rose into foothills and distant mountains. Boat after boat as far as he could see, stretching his neck over the edge, squinting against the sun. Next to him, in the rear of the boat, his mother was steering with an oar and looking after his smaller brother, Kanayuk, who sat on her back supported by the belt under her parka hood. He was busy sucking on a piece of dried meat tied to a stick by a sinew. In the stern Akiviak saw the gentle face of his grandfather, the old man standing slim and strong as he guided the boat with a long pole. In the middle of the boat, among the dogs, Akiviak's older brother Tigelok sat trying to scratch figures in a harpoon head with the aid of a pointed flint knife. Behind Tigelok sat his grandmother, together with his sister Sila, who was the eldest. They sat on a pile of sleeping skins on top of a large walrus hide which they used as a rain cover. The two of them were chewing on some pieces of seal leather which would later be used as soles for their mukluks. Akiviak's father was trudging wearily along the shore, driving the dogs that pulled the boat with long ropes of walrus hide. The ropes were so tight that they vibrated, singing with the strong currents of the river.

A gentle breeze moved down the hills and stirred the fluffy cotton grass on the marshes along the riverbank. The breeze carried with it the scent of the tundra. Birds twittered and whistled from the willow brush which flanked the river like a green hedge. Akiviak leaned back, and as he looked up into the blue sky he could see a huge black bird circling on motionless wings below a wisp of high sun-tinted clouds. He looked around and saw the brilliant light of the Arctic summer everywhere. The sun glittered on the water. In the tightly stretched translucent walrus hide which formed the bottom of the boat he could see a fine network of veins, like the nerves of a willow leaf. Through this translucent hide he could faintly see the pattern of waves rippling against the side of the boat. When he leaned over the edge and looked into the clear water, he could see small fish, like little arrows, darting among the stones on the bottom. A bright yellow butterfly settled on the steering oar, lifted its shiny wings, rested a while, and then moved out over the river. Akiviak wanted to call it back, for he thought that it would never reach the bank, tiny as it was in the middle of this vast expanse of water.

The boy moved closer to his mother and fell asleep. When he woke up the sun was about to set behind the mountains. His father made signs to camp for the night. The dogs were resting on the beach and licking their paws, sore from walking on the sharp stones in the sand.

In a small grassy clearing in the willow they pitched the tent and made camp. Akiviak, too young to be of any use, kept close to his grandfather, for he was the only one who seemed to have any time for him. When his grandfather moved into the brush, Akiviak followed. They returned with a bundle of long willow poles. These they stuck into the sand in a circle, the free ends tied together at the top, forming a domelike skeleton. Then they covered the frame with untanned caribou hides and the tent was made. Akiviak's mother brought in a wooden tray filled with dried caribou meat, which they shared and ate. They quenched their thirst with cold water from the river. Everyone burped politely, as if to indicate that they had had enough, and settled down to sleep. They slept side by side in the daylight between layers of caribou skin.

The journey continued. There were sunny days when the air was still and the mosquitoes swarmed like clouds around the boat. Akiviak kept swatting his face, killing mosquitoes by the hundreds until the palm of his hand was stained with his own blood. As the days passed and they moved upriver towards the mountains, the air became cooler, and was so clear that even the most distant mountains could be seen. But there were bitterly cold days when sleet and snow melted on their clothes and soaked through everything. Or the raindrops would freeze into icicles in the biting wind that hurtled against them from the mountain passes, as in darkest winter, even though it was still autumn. Akiviak shivered. The boat became heavier to move, the land more rugged, the banks steeper. It was difficult for the dogs to find a foothold in the slippery hillside or in the loose sand; at times earth and stones loosened and slid out into the river. Even though progress was painfully slow no one complained; not an unkind word was ever spoken. They just struggled on as if there were no choice, for they knew of no other way.

This was their world, the Northwest corner of what is now known as Alaska: the mountains around the watershed, the Utukok River to the west, the Umiat River to the north, and the Arctic coastline between the two. To the south were the vast forests, but none of them wanted to go there for it was dark and forbidding among the timber, and peopled with fierce warriors. To the east the mountains and the tundra continued indefinitely, but there was no reason to go there as long as they could remain where they were, and where they felt at home.

In the spring when they moved to the coast it was not merely because of the new season. It was an urge they felt for change, a need for something to look forward to—hunting seal, catching birds, bartering, the joy of meeting their kinsfolk at the coast. And there were practical reasons for leaving the tundra when the snow melted, for it was difficult to travel on the marshy flats when the sleds could no longer be used. It was better to drift to the sea on the river, where they could move about freely in their skin boats. But above all there was the craving for seafood. The fact that this food contained iodine needed for the sake of their health was unknown to them; they merely followed their natural instincts.

Their migrations were never dictated by time, as such, for the concept hardly existed. There were no watches or clocks; day was day, and night was night, it was all a matter of light. During the winter they were up and about as long as it was daylight. Before dark they prepared for the night, gathering around the oil lamps at dusk, telling tales and legends of the past. One story led to the next without interruption. It was all "Once upon a time," and time was of no consequence. Life was the same now as before, had been the same for generations, there was no difference. The only thing that mattered was the present, the very moment. And when their time on earth was over, existence would continue in some other form. Even though the body might be dead and buried, the soul would be released and transferred to another body, another person, perhaps a better one. At any rate there was nothing to fear.

They believed that the soul was immortal. This applied both to the name-soul, which eventually after one's death would be transferred to another person, and it applied to the soul which had to do with mind and knowledge. These loose-drifting spirits of their deceased forefathers might come to their rescue when there was trouble. It was therefore necessary to stay in their good graces, to seek their favor with gifts, to flatter them with praise, and to satisfy them with food and sacrifice if they were to have good luck in the hunt. They also believed that the soul of a living person could wander freely, but only during sleep. When sleep came, the soul would leave the sleeper's body; as soon as the soul returned he would wake up. Occasionally it happened that a soul would lose its way back, and arrive at the wrong host, so that one person got somebody else's soul by accident.

Their most important deity, the goddess Neqvivik, lived at the bottom of the sea. She reigned over all the game, and guided its migrations. For some reason, she had ruled that women were unsuited as hunters, and every time a woman went hunting the game disappeared. An act of punishment by the goddess, perhaps for disobeying her rules.

As long as they kept to the ancient customs and avoided all forms of taboo there was little to fear from the gods. This was not so with the evil spirits, especially the Kivitok trolls. They were always up to something bad. They would lurk around anywhere, disguised as all kinds of creatures. They might even take up their abode in peaceful people during bright daylight. It was the task of the shaman to master these evil spirits. This he did with the aid of his drum. He would beat the drum until he reached a state of trance, and then he could manipulate the evil spirits in or out of anything or anybody at will. Thus the shaman had much power and prestige. Not that the shaman was the only one that could communicate with the evil spirits, for ordinary people could, at times, get in some sort of touch with them. This happened during the drum dance, when they sang and danced, and occasionally transcended into a strange intoxicated state. Then the division between dream and reality disappeared and time ground to a halt, and past and present were one, indistinguishable. Some of the dancers had hallucinations, seeing and hearing things that were not real.

"O! how we will beat the drums and dance when we reach the watershed and meet our people!" thought Akiviak's father as he toiled ahead of the dogs along the river, bound for a winter on the tundra.

At last they arrived at the place in the mountains where the Utukok divided into two branches. One ran to the south through rugged terrain; it had many waterfalls and was most difficult to navigate with a large, heavily loaded skin boat. The other branch continued to the east through open landscape between distant mountains. But it was too shallow for the boat, so they carried the boat ashore, turned it upside down and left it on a rack. There were several boats there already, many people, and lots of tents.

They moved into a tent which they had used previously. Inside it was cozy and warm, the light filtering through a smoke vent in the ceiling. In the middle of the floor was a ring of stones used as a fireplace.

The older brother, Tigelok, was familiar with the area from

previous trips. He knew of a place in the river where their grandfather had taught him to catch trout with his bare hands. Now he took Akiviak with him to this place. In the middle of a large clump of sod which had slid out from the bank, and was resting on some large boulders, there was a hole. And in this hole they could clearly see the trout tightly packed, butting upstream against the turf, the light flashing from the silvery wriggling fish. Tigelok put his hand carefully down into the hole, placed it slowly over the tail of the nearest trout, and moved it forward until he reached the gills. Then he suddenly grasped and lifted the writhing trout out of the water. After a brief wait while the fish in the hole had quietened down again, Tigelok repeated the trick. He continued until he had enough for a meal. Then, to carry the catch more easily, a thin willow twig was threaded through the gills of the fish. They walked back to camp beaming with joy.

In front of the tent they found their grandfather sitting on a mound, working on a piece of flint. There were flint stones in a variety of colors all along the Utukok River. Akiviak had seen his father pick them up as he walked along the riverbank, pulling the boat. They were used for knives, arrowheads, spearheads and harpoon heads. Now the old man sat there with a round blue-gray flintstone in his hand. He turned it around, looked at it from all sides, examined it carefully to determine which way it would split. Then he took the large stone hammer with its handle of caribou antler, and split the stone into four pieces. Next he used a smaller hammer to shape the flint pieces to his liking. Finally he raised the flint chips at an angle and chiseled out the edges until they were sharp as a knife blade.

They broke camp, packing their belongings in skin bags strapped to the backs of their dogs, their sleeping skins tied to their own backs, spears and bows in their hands. They went on foot up the river. The dogs wobbled along in single file under the weight of the skin bags, their tails wagging in anticipation. Thus the procession undulated to the east over the tundra, tracing the contours of the land, around the high hills, up over gentle rising ridges, down the valleys, across a wilderness of swaying niggerheads. First came the grandfather, poking the ground with his long willow pole. Then the dogs, followed by the women and the children. At the very end came Akiviak's father, seeing to it that no one was left behind, for the walk was difficult.

At last they arrived at the place where the sleds had been left in the spring, resting on large stones by the riverbank.

It was a wide field of flat tundra above the shining waters of a long lake. Along a small stream which emptied into the lake, the willow brush grew only shoulder high. Beyond the stream the autumn-tinted tundra rose gently towards the foothills of the mountains: fields of gray and yellow lichen, blood-red blueberry heather, and shiny white cotton grass. An occasional thatch of withered grass swayed in the faint breeze among the green of dwarf birch and Arctic willow. Under this carpet of vegetation lived the rodents, the lemming and the ground squirrels, with their burrows and their trails. A solitary snow owl sat on a tuft of grass staring blindly into space with its pale yellow eyes. From the lake rose the cry of a loon.

On a hill above the brook they made camp. They pitched their tent next to the tent of Elijah, the brother of Akiviak's father. He was the shaman, the witch doctor with a strange wild look in his eyes. He was restless and moved as unpredictably as an ermine, thrusting his head forward when he walked. He always talked with a hoarse voice. His face was broad and bony, without any gentle features whatsoever. He had the habit of grinding his teeth, as if he were in constant pain. He would look at you with stone-gray cold eyes which never smiled.

While the women and children remained in camp, the men prepared for the caribou hunt. They lashed the packs onto the backs of their dogs and took off across the tundra towards the mountains. They carried their weapons: bows and arrows, throwing spears, daggers made of sharp caribou antlers.

Tigelok took Akiviak along to trap ground squirrels. There were lots of them on the slope above the lake in their burrows and underground tunnels. Every so often they appeared, poking their pointed noses out of an opening to take a look. Then they hurried back in again. Carefully, Tigelok fixed a snare made of stiff sinew outside the opening of a tunnel balancing it on a twig and fastening it securely to a stone. Then the boys hid themselves. When the ground squirrel came shooting out of its burrow it went straight into the snare and was caught. Ground-squirrel meat was all they had to eat for a while.

There were ptarmigan in the willows by the brook. They had already started to change color, and were now spotted and almost white on the wings. They spent most of the time cooing in the willows. There too Tigelok placed his snares. One day he caught a bird and Akiviak was allowed to carry it home. He tied it by its head to his belt, dragging the tail of the ptarmigan on the ground as he walked.

That year, in his fourth summer, Akiviak's grandfather made him his first bow, gave him a blunt arrow and taught him to shoot. When, in his excitement, the boy wanted to show his mother his new weapon, the arrow slipped and barely missed her head. His mother got quite a scare but refrained from scolding the boy, for there were visitors present, and to correct a child in front of others was to insult the child's soul. Nevertheless, Akiviak was ashamed and hurt. He hid the bow, and wandered off by himself behind the hill. There he lay on his back in the heather, listened to the wind that stirred the dried leaves of the dwarf birch, gazed into the sky in his loneliness. He watched the passing clouds, saw falcons flying high in the air, and he wondered how all this was made and who he really was. This occupied him for quite a while, and he thought to himself: "If I only could fly like the falcon, sail among the clouds, wing my way over the mountains to see what there is on the other side!" And thus he forgot his humiliation.

Suddenly a happy thought occurred to him: he recalled that he had left a ptarmigan snare standing in the willow behind the knoll. Now he heard something cooing in that direction. Perhaps he had caught a bird! Happily he jumped to his feet and took off for the willows. There was no ptarmigan in his snare, but now the voices of shouting children reached him. He followed the sounds and found a group of children playing outside Paneak's tent. The boys were throwing their spears against a target. This they did for a while until they lost interest and switched to shooting with bow and arrow until they had had enough of that, too. But the girls were sitting in a circle braiding sinew all the time, and never seemed to tire. Some other children were kicking a football made of caribou skin; they were the ones that made the most noise.

They kept it up until one of the children noticed something unusual taking place in Paneak's tent. People were rushing in and out of the tent; one of the women carried a wooden bucket filled with steaming hot water. One small girl lifted the bearskin which covered the doorway and peeped in, and at once all of the children gathered outside the door. Those nearest the opening could see Paneak's wife lying on her back on a pile of willow twigs in the middle of the floor. She appeared to be in pain. Elijah stood over her, trying to tie a string of sinew below her breasts. This was to stop the pain from spreading upwards to the rest of her body. Then one of the women came to chase the children away, but they remained in the vicinity, for they had a feeling that something was about to happen pretty soon. Then it came: the cry of a newborn child. Thus Timarok was born in a skin tent on the tundra.

One day the caribou hunters returned. Akiviak saw them as little dark specks far out on the tundra. The dogs had already sensed their coming. They raised their heads high in the air and howled, first one, then all of them joined in a chorus of howls. But there came no reply from the pack dogs out on the tundra, who were probably too tired to bother. But when the hunters reached the camp they were greeted with overwhelming joy. Everyone who could walk or crawl was there to meet them. Now the women took over, unloading the dogs, and tending to the game. They cut up the meat and placed it on drying racks high above the ground, well out of the reach of the dogs. They gathered all the long bones, placed them on a flat slab of stone, and crushed them with a stone hammer. Then the crushed bones were boiled in a wooden vessel in order to extract the marrow fat. Akiviak watched his mother build a fireplace of stones in the middle of the tent. She piled a stack of tiny twigs over a handful of dry moss, brought out her kindling tools, squatted down and started to move the bow back and forth until a burning smell came from the rubbing end of the stick, and a faint stream of smoke drifted from the rotating wooden pin. Suddenly a tiny magical blue flame popped up from the powdery moss near the end of the pin. She captured the flame with the aid of a wooden shaving and ignited the dry moss and twigs in the fireplace. Soon a fire was crackling in the middle of the tent. Akiviak's mother placed a heap of round stones in the fire; when they started to glow she picked them out, one by one, with a long prong made of caribou antlers. She dropped the red-hot stones into a wooden bucket filled with marrowbones and water. The stones caused the water to boil. Then the bucket was left to cool, at which time the fat was skimmed off the top and packed into a dried caribou stomach. This was then placed on the drying rack. During the winter the marrowbone fat would be cut into pieces and eaten together with meat on special festive occasions.

The days passed, as they always did. Gradually the air became cooler. The ground froze and there was hoarfrost on the heather. Ice formed on the lake.

One evening Akiviak went ice-fishing with his grandfather, using a hook made of bone tied to a line of sinew. It was bright moonlight, the sky full of stars, glowing with a faint northern light. The four-year-old kneeled down on the ice, which was smooth and clear as crystal. And there beneath him was a remarkable sight: he saw himself for the first time, mirrored in the ice. And in this picture of himself, he saw the reflection of the stars in the sky. Below it all, through the transparent ice, he saw schools of small fish that swarmed like a milky way of flickering lights. He was completely taken by this revelation. To him this was a miracle: the stars and the fish united in his own image. Something had happened inside him, perhaps, he thought, a religious awakening. Later he realized that this was the moment when he became fully aware of his own being, the first time he pictured himself as a part of all creation.

One day the snows came. Waking in his tent, Akiviak noticed the change the moment he opened his eyes. A strange light filtered through the translucent walrus stomach which served as a window. When he lifted the heavy bearskin covering the entry and came out of the tent, he saw that the whole landscape had changed. Shiny white fields sparkled in the sun. Snow-covered mountains beaconed in the distance. The footprints of a fox traced a perfectly straight line along the stream bed. Nothing moved in this white world of utter silence. When the raven cried in the mountains it sounded as if it listened for an answer between each cry. But only the echo returned.

This was the time of the long sled journeys. From now on they would always be on the move, like wolves following the caribou south across the tundra.

They got up long before dawn. Akiviak disliked to be awakened in the dark. Drowsy, he would sit on his sleeping skin feeling sorry for himself, chewing on a piece of frozen caribou meat, occasionally washing it down with a mouthful of cold water. Then with an effort, he started to dress. On his feet he wore caribou-skin socks, the hair facing in, and mukluks made of the skin from the legs of the caribou, the hair facing out. The soles were made of sealskin. Inside the mukluks were insoles of fur, the hairy side facing upwards. Next came two pairs of fur trousers—a pair of inner trousers with the hair facing in, and an outer pair with the hair facing out—and a double caribou parka. The mittens were made of fur, with short hair.

As soon as everyone was fully dressed they broke camp, loaded the sleds, and put on their snowshoes. The smaller children were placed on top of the load, and the dogs were hitched to the sleds. As a rule Akiviak's father harnessed himself to the sled and helped the dogs pull. His mother, carrying Akiviak's smaller brother Kanayuk on her back, guided the sled. Now and then she too had to help pull. When the snow was very deep and the going especially bad, the grandfather would take the younger children with him and walk ahead on foot, long before the rest of them started. He raced with the children in order to motivate them to move on. It was then easier for the dogs to follow their footprints, for they were eager to catch up with the children. When the dogs did catch up Akiviak was allowed to sit on the sled the rest of the way, and he would quickly fall asleep on top of the load. They always stopped for the night while it was still daylight.

In this way they struggled on, day after day in vain pursuit of the caribou. As the days passed they consumed their rations from the load, thus lightening the burden of the dogs.

Eventually they reached the pass where the caribou crossed the mountains, the herds moving south towards the forests in the fall, and north towards the Arctic Ocean in the spring. To this place the same group of families returned every year and settled down for the winter's camp. Because they were to remain for a long period of time, great pains were taken to make the tents as comfortable as possible. Caribou skins from which the hair had been removed were used as covers for the tents. The skins were pulled over a dome-shaped frame of willow poles. For windows they used the scraped stomach skin of walrus or bearded seal which they had carried with them. These windows were translucent, but not transparent. In the ceiling there was a small vent allowing the smoke to escape. A large bearskin covered the entrance to the tent, the hairy side facing out. It was fixed above the door opening, and when left hanging naturally it covered the opening perfectly. As they entered or left the tent they simply lifted the edge of the skin, which then would fall back in place by itself. Stone lamps burned blubber oil for light. The flame was adjusted by varying the width of the wick, which was made of dried moss. Against the walls of the tent were the sleeping skins, which during the day were used as seats. At night they rolled the skins onto the floor, which was strewn with twigs, lay down side by side, and covered themselves with fur. In this way they kept warm and felt safe.

One night Akiviak awakened. The light of the moon shone through the window and fell upon his face. Everyone else around him was asleep; some were snoring, others talked in their sleep. His father was grinding his teeth, tossing about in the throes of a nightmare. Akiviak moved closer to his grandfather.

Suddenly the dogs began to bark. The barking was different from the usual friendly greeting when visitors approached the camp. Akiviak's father grabbed his spear and went outside to see what the matter was. By now the rest of the family had awakened. They sat up and listened. The barking stopped. Akiviak's father came back and said that he had seen nothing. He looked pale.

Then he picked out a glowing twig from the fireplace and lit the oil lamp. Men from the neighboring tents came in and gathered around the fire. They talked for a while. Finally the grandfather got up and joined the circle of talking men. The lamplight fell upon his face. As the men moved, their shadows formed grotesque figures on the wall.

Then the old man started to tell his tales.

"Ai, ai," chanted the men.

"We were hunting caribou one winter, about this time of the year, my brother and I and the old man, Tunga, from Umiat. We spent the night in a snowhouse in the mountains north of here. Tunga had been behaving so strangely, was depressed and hot-tempered, said he could hear voices inside his body; he was sure that they were evil spirits who wanted to hurt him. He said that he had seen the footprints of strangers in the snow during the day. In the middle of the night we were awakened by the dogs. We thought we could hear footsteps in the snow. Tunga grabbed his spear and went out. He never came back."

"Ai-ai," cried Elijah, and sounded more hoarse than usual.

Akiviak slept and dreamt that he walked out of the tent with his spear; he walked all through the night and came to a canyon where a strong wind was blowing, whipping the snow down the valley; the wind got hold of him and swept him off; he was caught in an avalanche of blowing snow, he heard the roar of caribou bulls, of thundering hooves, the heavy breathing of a herd that galloped through the storm down the valley like a rising sea of beasts. A passing buck carried a midget man, a Kivitok, on its head. The midget was holding on to the antlers with one hand, waving at Akiviak with the other. Then suddenly Akiviak was lifted off the ground once again with the howling wind, and he landed on the back of a buck. Thus he rode with the herd in a thundering gallop down the valley and out over the tundra, all the way to the coast. As the sun rose the wind died, the blizzard ceased and the whole herd dissipated like the morning mist in the rising sun. Now Akiviak found himself on the edge of the sea ice. Suddenly he saw the head of a large whale appear out of the sea. It stayed there for a moment, staring at him. In the cold eyes of the beast he saw its soul like a faintly glowing fire, a shimmering light that rose and fell with the breathing of the whale.

Akiviak opened his eyes and saw the tiny flame of the blubber lamp flickering in the draft. Surrounding the flame was a glistening rainbow of water vapor from Elijah's breath as he told his tales:

He was out on the ice, standing by a breathing hole, ready to strike the seal with his harpoon as soon as it appeared. But instead of a seal, the head of a polar bear suddenly came through the hole. The bear dived, then reappeared, and by now Elijah could clearly see that this was no ordinary bear. It was much larger than any bear he had ever seen, and instead of four legs it had ten, five on either side. Suddenly it dawned on him that this probably was the dread kukuweaq, the ten-legged bear. Frightened, he looked around for a place to hide. Among the pack ice he discovered two large slabs standing on end and leaning against each other at the top, like a tent. The opening between the two slabs was barely wide enough for him to crawl into. He ran as fast as he could and quickly crawled into the crack. The bear came after him. It tried to force itself into the crack which became narrower the farther it went. The bear roared and pushed on until it almost got hold of Elijah. But then the bear got stuck. It could move neither forward nor backward. Elijah quickly crawled out on the other side, ran around the hummock and rammed his harpoon through the rectum of the bear all the way into its heart. At that very moment a spark of the northern lights slashed the sky like a bolt of lightning, splitting the ice. The bear lay stretched out in the snow. It was dead.

By now Akiviak had fallen asleep again. He dreamt that he was lying on the ice, and saw the curtains of the northern lights waving in broad sweeps across the sky. Suddenly the veil of a trailing aurora swooped down and took his soul and lifted it into the heavens. There he saw a group of children in colorful costumes; they held hands and danced like a train of glittering lights all the way from the horizon to the hills.

In this way Akiviak lived through the night, in transition between dream and reality. The legends he heard while awake he elaborated on in his sleep, thus more or less erasing the distinction between fact and fiction in his mind. This developed his vivid imagination. Often he would talk to himself, or think aloud. At times, when he was quiet, he could sense a kind of conversation taking place within himself, as if there were several souls in his mind talking to one another. As a rule one was in favor, and one opposed, to whatever Akiviak had in mind. When it grew dark he was afraid, but so were the others, it seemed; for like himself the rest of them kept closer together in the night when they went to sleep. Thus they found safety in each other while they waited for the day.

One day Akiviak's brother Tigelok and another boy went out to hunt ptarmigan with bow and arrow. Akiviak followed them. They had walked quite a distance when they unexpectedly saw a caribou, a solitary buck feeding undisturbed in the distance. Its antlers gleamed like red-hot metal in the sun as it lifted its head high. The boys asked Akiviak to go home; they would try to get the buck. They ran to get within range of the caribou and left Akiviak standing on the tundra. Akiviak was frightened. There were probably wolves around; surely they would kill him. He started to run after the boys. He slipped and stumbled in his little snowshoes, crying all the way. He broke through the thin ice as he was crossing a frozen stream and got his feet wet. His brother happened to see him and came to his rescue. He stroked the boy's chin and said that if he stopped crying he could come with them after all, providing he kept absolutely quiet. Then Tigelok showed Akiviak how to get down as soon as the caribou raised its head for a look. They succeeded in getting within range of the buck and they killed it with one arrow, even though it was a large buck.

The mountain pass where Akiviak's people had their camp

had always been a major hunting ground for caribou. At the water's divide, where the valley opened into the Arctic plain from the south, the terrain rose in a gentle incline to a little knoll which, on the far side, dropped off sharply. On top of this knoll the hunters had placed their caribou snares for as long as anyone could remember. A typical snare was a loop of thin skin rope spread out between willow poles. The free end of the snare rope was securely fastened to a large stone. Several rows of snares were placed one behind the other. Around the edges of the knoll the hunters had stationed bundles of willow twigs, forming a sort of corral. The bundles were tied together by skin rope, and resembled the shape of a man. These bundles were placed upright in the snow around the knoll a few yards apart. From there they were arranged in two rows, flaring out like a funnel for five miles down the valley.

One day a large herd of caribou was seen coming up the valley. From a distance it resembled an anthill; it looked as if the entire valley was alive: an undulating mass moving slowly up the hillside. The animals were surrounded by a cloud of icy fog caused by the warm moist breath that they expired into the cold air around them. A gentle breeze was blowing in the valley, away from the herd.

This sight caused a sudden commotion. The Eskimo's cry, "Tuttu" (meaning "caribou"), echoed through the pass, and the entire camp sprang to life. Two of the boys, the best runners, were sent down into the valley behind the herd. They were to drive the herd up toward the opening of the corral. Meanwhile the hunters, together with the older children, gathered behind the willow bundles on both sides of the corral. There they hid themselves, keeping absolutely quiet, watching the approaching herd. The smaller children were concealed among the large stones behind Akiviak's grandfather, who had placed himself a short distance below the knoll. He was on guard, and was to give the signal to the hunters at the proper time. He collected the children and took cover behind a rock. Akiviak was trembling with excitement. Now they could see that the runners had reached the herd. Apparently the caribou had gotten wind of the boys, for they were restless, and started to move more quickly up the valley. Now they were abreast of the funnel opening formed by the two spreading rows of willow sheaves. But they kept their distance, probably because of the sheaves' resemblance to human beings. Suddenly the runners started to shout, their cries echoing back and forth between the mountains. This immediately caused the herd to take off in full gallop up the valley, between the rows of willow bundles, straight into the corral on the hill. They came in a thunderous gallop, their hooves pounding against the frozen ground. It felt as if the entire tundra was shaking. As soon as the herd had passed the spot where the grandfather was hiding, he jumped up and shouted, so that it echoed in the valley: "Sii-ai!"

This was the signal for the hunters to come out of hiding. Suddenly they all popped up, followed by the children, and drove the terrified beasts straight into the snares. Those animals that escaped the snares continued galloping over the hill and plunged to their deaths into the stony slope below. In this way almost the entire herd was captured, for very few of the animals escaped.

Now the hunters leaped forward with their spears and their daggers made of caribou antler and killed the trapped animals. Soon the women came with the pack dogs to help carry the meat home.

The caribou kill had secured enough meat to last through the winter. As soon as the sun started to melt the snow on the southern slopes, they headed west for the coast. They traveled at night when the frozen snow was strong enough to carry the weight of the sled, they slept and rested their dogs during the day. In this way they made good progress and were able to travel comfortably, sitting on the sleds much of the time.

As time passed the days grew longer. Then at long last came the bright spring days, with the blue of the evening fading into twilight late in the night. Now they became restless; a longing for the life by the coast filled their minds. The sparrows whistled in the willow, little scruffy bundles of feathers shivering in the icy Arctic wind.

Then one day the first flock of geese winged its way north across the mountains. The sight of the migratory birds excited the dogs. They strained against their harnesses and pulled for all they were worth, leaving bloody footprints from their paws, which were cut raw by the sharp icicles in the crusted snow.

Finally the travelers reached the place where they had left their skin boats in the fall. Here they waited until the river ice broke up. It started suddenly, after a spell of hot weather. In the course of the day the water level of the river kept rising, lifting the ice, which eventually broke loose from land and split up into floes. By the evening the larger floes began to crack and the pieces of ice drifted swiftly down-stream and piled up at a narrow part of the river. Above this point the water rose as new floes continued to pile up. Then suddenly, in the middle of the night, this huge mass of ac-cumulated ice broke loose with a roar, a raging mass of ice and water churning down to the sea.

As soon as the river was clear, they put the skin boats on the water and drifted down to the coast. In the long, narrow lagoon, the kaseqaluk, inside the sandspit where they always had their summer camp, the ice was still unbroken and blocked their way. But they simply pulled the umiaks onto the ice, hitched up the dogs, and pulled the boats, fully loaded, on slippery ivory runners straight across the lagoon ice. They landed on the sandspit, at a place known as Vivak, which means "a place to return to." Beyond the sandspit, the sea ice extended unbroken for as far as they could see, but along the shore there was a lane of open water caused by the tide.

Inside a ring of stones facing the sea, they put up their tents in their traditional places, hung their caribou meat on the old drying racks, and established a comfortable summer camp. The number of tents steadily increased as the inland people came down from the mountains. There must have been no less than twenty tents altogether. (Akiviak, like the rest of his people, was unable to count to more than twenty. They had only ten fingers and ten toes, and this was, in their language, "a whole person to the end.")

Before the sea ice broke up, Akiviak hunted birds with the other children. They would hide behind a hummock and wait; when a flock of auklets or ducks came flying close above the ice, they threw their birdslings. The sling consisted of a braided string of sinew about six feet long, cut from the long back muscle of the caribou. A small stone was tied to each end of the string. As the birds approached, the hunters would swing the string like a lasso over their heads and throw it into the flock. With luck the string would wind around one of the birds, which would then lose its balance and fall to the ground. It had to be caught quickly, before it could regain consciousness and take off.

Then there was the seal hunt. Early one morning Akiviak was out with Tigelok, pulling the kayak along the ice on a small sled. Several seals were swimming in the open water at the edge of the ice. Tigelok carefully lowered the kayak into the sea, arranged the harpoon, fixed the float, placed himself in the delicate craft, and paddled away. Akiviak remained with the sled, watching. He was so excited and eager that he shivered as he stood, following every move his brother made. Now Tigelok stopped paddling. He placed his oar in the container on top of the kayak, lifted the harpoon out of its forked holder, where it was kept when not in use, and checked the rope attaching the harpoon head to the float. Then, motionless, he waited. Suddenly a seal appeared just ahead of him, only a few yards away. Tigelok thrust the harpoon into the back of the seal. There was a terriffic splash. A spray of gushing water poured down on the hunter. The waves caused by the seal's sudden motion rocked the tiny craft as the wounded animal dived, pulling the harpoon line with it. Tigelok quickly threw the float, which was fastened to the end of the line, overboard. The seal had already dived so deep that the line was taut, and was now pulling the float partly under water. Tigelok followed every move, and kept his eye fixed on the float. He had put his oar in the water, and kept his kayak close to the float. Then the seal came up to breathe. It was bleeding, the sea dyed red where it surfaced, and there was foam around its nostrils. It dived again. Tigelok eyed the float. Gradually the seal lost its strength; it came rising slowly to the surface and remained floating on its back.

From a distance Akiviak watched his brother attach a towline to the seal. Now Tigelok came paddling towards the edge of the ice with his prize behind him. In his excitement Akiviak jumped up and down on the ice. He ran in circles, and hardly knew what to do with himself. But when he was told to take the towline and hold the seal while his brother crawled out of the kayak, he calmed down. They hauled the seal up onto the ice and dragged it home.

This was Tigelok's first seal. He approached the village, pulling his catch, head thrust forward, his hands grasping the rope behind him, pulling until his body was almost parallel with the ground. He kept his eyes fixed on the ground a few paces ahead, struggling with his burden. Every so often his sealskin mukluks slipped on the ice. Akiviak trailed behind, dragging the kayak on the little sled.

Many men had gathered on the beach, but Tigelok pretended not to notice. He kept on pulling until he reached his tent. There he left the seal in front of the door.

"Here you are," he said to his mother.

He calmly collected his skin rope and moved away as if nothing had happened.

The event called for a feast in honor of the young hunter on the occasion of his first kill. The women set out to butcher the seal and boil the meat. They piled it onto wooden trays and prepared an eating orgy for the entire village.

The men came first and took their seats in the karigi, or dance tent. Then came the women and the children. Those who could find no seat remained outside the tent. Tigelok himself was the center of attention. But he did not touch the meat. This was their custom, as if to show that the young boy had now become a provider, and was no longer dependent.

While the hunters helped themselves and praised the meat, complimenting the able young hunter on the superb seal he had caught, they questioned him, in keeping with an old tradition, about the hunt: how the seal had behaved, where the harpoon had hit, and how long it took before the seal had given in.

The women sat by themselves as onlookers, eating silently. Not that they were inferior to the men in any way; if anything, it was the other way around. The fact was, however, that hunting was the responsibility of the men. The women had other duties—among them making good hunters out of their men. And this they accomplished in their own subtle way, not by talking.

Akiviak's grandfather served as the master of ceremonies. He praised the luck of the young hunter. Then everyone tried to outdo one another in expressing their praise and their joy. The father of the young hunter exclaimed, "Isn't this what I have always said? Tigelok was born a great hunter!" Tigelok's eyes filled with tears. Then everyone praised the seal, which had meat so tasty and so tender that it almost melted in the mouth. None of them had ever tasted anything like it, they proclaimed. For Akiviak it was all a joke until he realized that it was indeed a show put on in accordance with tradition.

Then it was Tigelok's turn. He had to describe in detail all that had happened, from start to finish: what he had thought, what he had done. The rest of them questioned and probed and interrogated him as if none of them had ever participated in a seal hunt before.

When the entire seal had been consumed, the mother of the hunter collected all the bones. She handed them over to Tigelok, who then walked with the guests in a procession, headed by Akiviak's grandfather, down to the beach. Here they all gathered in a circle around Tigelok by the open lead between the land and the sea ice. Tigelok kneeled down and dropped the bones carefully into the sea. The crowd around him watched the ceremony with reverence. In their minds they had merely borrowed the meat of the seal, but its soul had not been touched. Now the soul was free to come back to pick up the old bones. Then all the soul had to do was to put meat on the bones again, and there was a new seal for them to catch. Obviously, it would please the soul to hear them boast about the meat. And then they made it clear that the seal had landed in such good hands, and that its meat was so greatly appreciated, that it would be in the best interest of the animal's soul to be caught again by the same hunter. Especially when the hunter was so skilled, and so gentle.

"Ai, ai," cried Elijah, the witch doctor.

By this time the sea ice had started to break completely loose. It broke into large floes and drifted to the south. Soon the coast would be clear and the Eskimos from the villages farther south could come up by boat to barter. For their caribou meat, tallow, and hides the inland Eskimos expected to trade from their coastal cousins what they needed of whale blubber for their lamps, maktaq (the skin of the narwhale) for their feasts, and skins of bearded seals for the soles of their boots. It was now time to prepare for the arrival of their kinsfolk from the coast. They erected the large dance tent on the sandspit, kept an eager watch from the beach, and waited.

One day there came a cry from the brink:

"They are coming!"

The whole village quickly assembled around the dance tent. The drummers got out their drums, made of walrus stomach stretched over a circular frame of driftwood, which they banged with a stick. There were five drummers in all. They started to chant, then beat the drums. Their song rose and fell with the monotonous rhythm of the drums. Now four of the women lined up in front of the drummers, dressed in their colorful ceremonial parkas trimmed with ermine fur. The procession started towards the beach. First came the dancing women, followed by the drummers, then the rest of the inland Eskimos, a jubilant mass, shuffling their feet in the sand.

They caught sight of a convoy of some eight to ten skin boats out at sea, moving slowly up the coast. Now as they approached the beach, the women at the oars suddenly started to row as fast as they could. The very moment the first boat touched the sandy beach the drummers stopped, as if by signal. The eldest of the inland Eskimos stepped forward to welcome the visitors. The headman in the boat sent gifts ashore with instructions as to who was to receive them. There was narwhal skin for Akiviak's uncle Paneak, a piece of bearded sealskin for Akiviak's father, and a walrus tusk for his grandfather. In return, the visitors were invited to the karigi for the traditional feast and drum dance. Then they were helped to unload their umiaks.

With much shouting and jubilation the guests were escorted into the tent and shown their honored seats on the caribou skins along the walls. The host women took the guests' parkas and hung them under the ceiling to dry. Each guest was given a wisp of dried grass with which to dry his feet. Then everyone settled down and started to converse. To begin with, according to custom, the guests praised the friendship, said how nice it was to be in such an excellent tent. The hosts replied by praising the gifts they had received, by remarking on how well the guests looked, and what fine boats they had. Then the conversation turned to wind and weather, the migration of game, the hunting of whale and the performance of the sled dogs. Akiviak listened. He was seated with the rest of the children on the floor by the door.

While the men talked, the women made ready for the big feast to come, dishing up one course after the other. First they served dried fish, then dried seal meat, then raw auklets, followed by dried caribou meat served with bone marrow and berries mixed with blubber oil in caribou stomachs. The eating seemed to take forever, but finally they were finished and started to prepare for the dance. The coastal Eskimos began. They twisted and turned to the rhythm of the drums in the middle of the crowded karigi. While they danced they tossed gifts about; they were small gifts, tokens of friendship, such as pieces of sinew, bits of fur, maktaq and meat.

When the guests had finished and were cooling off, it was the Utukok people's turn to dance. For several days they continued in this way, taking turns to dance in the summer camp at Icy Cape where the inland and coastal people met to barter.

One day, while one of the boat crews was out hunting, they discovered a whale floating in the drift ice. They approached it cautiously and discovered that it was dead. This was strange, since none of them had been hunting whale that year. However, a whale was a whale; perhaps it was sent to them as a gift by the gods.

They fastened lines to the whale and towed it to land. There was tremendous excitement when those keeping watch by the village caught sight of the umiak towing the whale. Their shouts rang from the brink. The cry was repeated by those who were running about among the tents.

Suddenly the beach was full of people who jumped and yelled, waving their arms and running about in circles. Before their eyes a mountain of meat came floating in from the sea.

They brought out their broad-bladed slate knives and started to flense the whale. The women were in charge, and the men gave a helping hand here and there as required. Akiviak too helped to carry the meat. They worked standing in the water. As they gradually dug their way into the whale, their attention was drawn to the wound, where there were masses of coagulated blood. And there, in the middle of the whale, they found a harpoon of a kind they had never seen before. It was much larger and heavier than their own harpoons, with large distending barbs. The coastal people thought that the whale had been killed by those foreigners known to their cousins further south on the coast.

Elijah took the harpoon and threw it out into the sea.

Akiviak had never before seen so much food gathered in one place, an endless supply of meat and blubber. But finally it was all placed on the racks to dry, and it was time to celebrate with a blanket toss, or maluktak. Everyone gathered around a walrus skin. The strongest of the men grabbed hold of the edges of the skin and pulled it tight as a drum. Then one of the young boys jumped on. The men pulled and tightened the skin, and the boy bounced high up into the air; he landed on his feet, only to be thrown into the air again. He went so high that Akiviak thought he would never come down. But when he finally did, he landed outside the skin and broke his collarbone. Even so everybody laughed.

Now they could face the days ahead without concern, for their larders were filled. They could really enjoy life. Now all they did was barter. And when the sun was high and the summer was at its warmest, the coastal people returned to their boats and paddled away. And the Utukok people started on their journey to the tundra, to their hunting grounds amidst the mountains.

III

THE CHANGE

THE years passed, times changed. The small tribe of inland Eskimos, the Nunamiuts, roamed about as before. They continued to swing back and forth between the coast in the summer and the tundra in the winter. This way they always had something to look forward to.

In the year of Akiviak's seventh summer, as they were on their way back to the mountains, their lives changed abruptly.

The fall had come particularly early that year, with an endless succession of gales and blizzards. Then the weather turned mild; it started to rain and the tundra was covered with a solid sheet of ice. This caused the caribou to seek their food elsewhere in distant pastures. The few that remained were so starved that they were hardly worth killing. They were nothing but skin and bone.

Akiviak's father had predicted a lean year. The meals were few and far between; there were days when there was nothing to eat at all. Akiviak often went to bed on an empty stomach, dreaming about food. The dogs grew more emaciated and sickly every day, and dragged their feet. They were let loose to roam around and hunt on their own. They dug through the icecovered moss for ground squirrels and lemming. They chased snow owls, but caught none. In the end they survived on carrion. Then one day one of the dogs went mad, howling like a wild beast. It attacked the other dogs, going for their throats like a wolf. Then it turned lame, and died. Soon some of the other dogs became ill in this fashion. In the end there were only three dogs left.

Without dogs it was difficult to live on the tundra. With their livelihood gone, and without any means of transportation, Akiviak's people had no choice but to head for the coast.

Accompanied by Elijah's family they headed west, towards the sea. But there was a long way to go, and even though the load was light it was hard to walk on an empty stomach. They pulled all their belongings on their sleds, limping ahead, a piteous flock staggering across the tundra. Akiviak's father led the way; behind him came Tigelok and his grandfather, pulling the sled in silence. Akiviak's sister Sila steadied the load; his grandmother trotted along behind the sled, giving a hand every time the sled got stuck. Akiviak's youngest brother was on top of the sled, whimpering and looking miserable. His mother was pushing the sled. Akiviak walked by her side, holding on to the sled as he walked, dragging his stuffed baby sealskin behind him. It pained him to see his mother's face. Her eyes looked like caves deep in her skull. She looked pale, almost gray, but her cheeks were red in patches. She had a terrible cough, and once in a while she brought up blood. But she never complained. She just kept walking, pushing the sled for all she was worth. Akiviak himself wobbled along in a daze. He had difficulty keeping up with the rest of the group. He saw them as they rose and fell in the haze, the way he had seen distant islands in an arctic mirage. Hunger pains played havoc with his intestines; he tried to relieve the agony by chewing on the end of a skin rope. At times he just wanted to lie down in the snow, not to struggle any more. He wished that the day would soon come to an end so that they could stop for the night. As in a dream he saw snowhouses nestled snugly on a slope below the hills, saw the light from the burning oil lamps, the steam rising from the wooden vessels filled with boiling marrowbones. He could smell the blubber, taste the tender boiled seal meat. He dreamed that he ate and he ate. He lost himself so completely in his hallucinations that he was no longer aware of what was happening around him. He had lost his hold on the sled, and now he was far behind the others. With an extreme effort he tried to run to catch up, but his legs refused to obey him. Soon the group ahead of him was only a speck in the snow. He considered dropping the stuffed seal he was dragging along, but could not make himself do so. The last thing he would do was abandon the baby seal, which he would carry back to the sea, to be caught anew as soon as the boy was old enough. He struggled, slid on his slippery sealskin mukluks, fell, got up again. Then he saw his chance: an uphill slope, an incline towards a mountain pass. It appeared that the sled was slowing down. Those who were pulling had to stop and take a break. Akiviak mustered all the strength in his frozen limbs and dragged himself along. Now he was getting closer. This gave him new strength. Finally he caught up with the sled, too exhausted to show what he felt.

As they rested there on the sled, their backs turned against the biting wind, there came an explosion from the mountain behind them. But Akiviak was too drained to care, or even to think. But then he caught a glimpse of his grandfather's face. It frightened him, so he turned to see a roaring, thundering mass of snow hurtling down the mountain slope towards them. The terrified bodies on the sled did not move. There was a rush of air, followed by a rise in pressure so violent that everything loose on the sled was swept away. Then the avalanche subsided, and came to a halt in a depression along the river. A huge slab of rock bounded down the slope only a few paces behind the sled.

Where the avalanche had struck, the bare slope looked like a broad black band extending all the way to the top of the mountain. Above this, at the very top, columns of rocks stood on end, like jagged teeth against the sky. High up among the stones Akiviak could see something stirring, then it disappeared. His grandfather jumped from the sled. He said that what they had seen were the evil mountain spirits, the Kivitoks, who were dangerous. They had to hurry up to get away in time.

It appeared as if their common enemy had given them renewed strength, the strength of fear. They harnessed themselves to the sled and pulled as if it were a matter of life or death for them to get away. Past the ridge the landscape sloped gently down to the other side. Here the going was better, and the children were allowed to ride on the sled. Their mother stood on the runners behind the sled and steered.

Then all of a sudden the grandfather stopped the sled. He pointed towards a hillock to the right. There, above the willow brush, Akiviak caught sight of a caribou, a buck moving slowly uphill. Elijah and his family were already far ahead; they had probably disturbed the buck as they passed. The grandfather and Tigelok grabbed their bows and arrows and took off for the hills. They followed the stream all the way to the willows. But as the hunters became visible on the other side of the thicket, the caribou disappeared behind the crest of the hill. Then the hunters went out of sight behind the knoll.

The rest sat on the sled, waiting. Akiviak fell asleep. Suddenly he was startled awake by someone shouting. At once, fully awake, he sat up, pushed the parka hood away from his face and looked around. The hunters appeared over the crest of the hill, carrying heavy loads on their shoulders. Akiviak jumped to his feet, eager and hungry, ready with the rest of the children to rush up the hill to meet the hunters. They all grabbed the sled and pulled it up to the thicket as the hunters came down and dropped their catch of fresh meat in the snow. Immediately everyone dived in with their slate knives to cut chunks of meat off the bones. They chewed the tough meat and swallowed it raw. But they all too soon discovered there is a very limited amount of food on a starved caribou, even though they meticulously consumed every part of it, save the bones and the hide. They opened the guts in order to eat their contents as well, but found, to their amazement, nothing but moulted caribou hair in the stomach—an indication that there was something wrong with the buck, they feared. However, there were numerous larvae under the skin, especially over the hindquarter, as was commonly the case with the caribou. These larvae were now consumed with a ravenous appetite. That evening they went to sleep without hunger pains for the first time in a long while.

The following day they caught up with Elijah's sled. Together the two families continued westward toward the watershed where they had left their skin boats the previous year. It was easy to pull the sleds on their slick ivory runners over the hard frozen snow crust, barely covered with newly fallen snow less than an inch deep. The grandfather, who appeared quite fit now, decided to take off to the watershed on his own and look for caribou on his way. He packed his sleeping skins on his back, took his bow and arrow and his throwing spear, and set out along the foothills to the north. The rest continued down the tundra, which sloped gently to the west. In the afternoon the fog settled over the plains. They stopped, cut blocks out of the hard packed crusted snow and built a snowhouse. Akiviak could not resist the temptation: he scooped out some of the snow from the wall of the igloo to make snowballs which he threw at his sister Sila. He kept on until he had made a hole right through the wall. His mother mended the wall, and no one scolded the boy for his mischief.

They settled down in their snowhouse and waited, but the

grandfather failed to appear. Soon it was dark, but still there was no sign of the old man. The night passed, yet no sign of the missing hunter. This was strange, for he had appeared strong and healthy when he left, and would have had no reason to leave them to die. Evidently something must have happened to him —an accident, perhaps, or maybe the evil Kivitoks of the mountains had killed him. The grandmother, on the other hand, was of the opinion that he would be able to look after himself in any case. Nevertheless they started to search. They pulled the sleds with them over the hills, criss-crossing the landscape. Late in the afternoon they found the old man's footprints in the snow. They followed the tracks until nightfall, built an igloo and spent the night there. The next day they came upon the place where he had spent the night sheltered by a semicircular wall of snow blocks. Behind this wall he had rested on his sleeping skins; this was evident from the marks in the snow. They continued to follow his tracks to the west. But then it started to snow, and the tracks vanished. By late afternoon visibility had become so poor that they had to camp for the night in a snowhouse built jointly for the two families. In the course of the night the weather improved, and the following morning they continued to the west. By now they had given up any hope of finding the grandfather, so they followed the stream and sought the easiest route to the west.

As the days passed Akiviak began to recognize the country, the rocks and the willow brush along the river. Finally one day, exhausted and starving, they staggered down to the place where they had left their skin boat and found the grandfather sleeping in a snowhouse. Apparently he had been lost in the fog, had found his way by following the snowdrifts, but had come too far north and passed the divide unknowingly. Eventually he had found his bearings, turned back, and arrived at the boat place shortly before they did.

The previous fall they had left some seal blubber hanging on the drying racks. At that time it was too rancid to eat, so they had left it hanging for the dogs. Now they were glad to have it, though they suffered stomach-ache and diarrhea as a consequence; but rather this than starve.

One day there came a sad-looking crew down from the tundra, with a single dog harnessed in front of the sled. It was Paneak, the brother of Akiviak's mother, and his family. They were in dreadful shape; they had barely survived on the few snow owls and ptarmigan which they caught. Soon more families came down from the mountains. Most of them had been sick, some had died and were left wrapped in skins on the drying racks in the tundra. The survivors were now on their way to the coast. Many were leaving the mountains for good.

They remained in this camp until the river ice broke up. They lived on what little game they caught, and shared the catch equally. It was an emaciated, sorry-looking lot that eventually reached the coast. There they jiggered some fish through holes in the ice, harpooned an occasional seal, and caught eider ducks in flight with the aid of bird slings. The ice remained landfast for a long time that year. Elijah brought out his weather stone and called for the offshore wind to push the ice floes to the sea. This seemed to help, for one fine day there was sufficient open water to allow the umiaks to pass north along the land, towards the village of Nuvuk. On a sandspit up the coast they met a family in a sod house. As they approached, the father of the house came out. He was reluctant to let them in; evidently he feared that they might cause trouble in case they were involved in a family feud. By allowing them to enter his house he, according to custom, would have granted the visitors his protection and thus taken sides. But the woman of the house came out with a steaming wooden bowl filled with boiled meat. This they ate seated in the sand, but because of the chilling wind the food was cold by the time they had finished.

It was then that Akiviak realized that his father was ill. He had been ailing for some time; he was certainly no longer anything like the man he had been. He no longer led the way, or carried the brunt of the burden, but rather saved himself and looked for the easy way out. Now Akiviak noticed a boil on the man's neck the size of a small fist. He saw that his father had difficulty swallowing his food.

They continued along the coast to the north, hunting every time the opportunity presented itself, but catching very little. Eventually they arrived at a place where an old man lived by himself in a sod house. They waited outside for a long time. Finally Akiviak's father climbed up on the roof and called through the skylight to indicate their presence. When no one answered they entered the hut. Akiviak's father led the way, the rest following behind him. They entered through a square opening high on the outer wall. It was covered by a wooden shutter without hinges or handle, but fitted with a hole large enough to put a finger through to remove it from the frame. They came into a hallway with walls made of stacked blocks of sod. Crawling through a trapdoor at the far end of the hallway, they came into the main room. It had an elevated wooden floor and a wide bunk covered with caribou skins. Here a man was sitting, holding a broad-bladed stone knife in his hand. He pressed it into a crack in the wall, then turned to them in silence.

Akiviak's father spoke. He said that they were hungry. The man hesitated, then said that there was no food in the house. The course of the conversation, however, revealed that he did have a ringed seal. The trouble was that he had killed the seal with a new kind of weapon which would bring bad luck. He brought out the weapon, and tried to describe it: "You see a stock and a barrel, which is loaded from the end, and when you pull the trigger it makes a bang and shoots a bullet along." He had bartered this firestick, in exchange for a dog from a trapper who came from the south.

Elijah became quite disturbed, said he could smell something bad and insisted that the dead seal should not be touched. But Akiviak's father was stubborn and too starved to control his hunger. He helped himself to the meat and ate a great deal while the rest of them watched. Elijah was furious: "This you should never have done!" he cried.

They paddled northward in their umiak. And then one day at sundown they saw something odd: on a large floe of old ice lay a strange object, a boat made of wood with masts and sails no less than 20 times the size of an umiak. It had toppled over and was lying on its side on the ice, drifting with the wind.

They moved closer, watched, paddled a bit further, stopped, kept their oars still in the water and looked again; they saw no sign of life. They rested on the oars, and waited. But no life of any kind could be detected, neither on the ship nor on the floe. They paddled a little further, cautiously; no one said a word, not knowing what to believe or what to do. By now they could clearly distinguish the details. The sails were torn; they fluttered like ghosts in the slack rigging. A door had been left ajar. It moved to and fro with the wind, squeaked and jarred as it swung back and forth, and cried like a ptarmigan calling in the willow back home. There was no other sound, apart from the wind which whimpered and rattled in the rigging. There was an air of horror about the whole thing. They sat in the boat, their mouths wide open, staring. Elijah was the first to get hold of himself. He turned his head, and spoke in a hoarse whisper: "Here I see danger. We must get away."

They grabbed the oars and rowed with powerful and cautious strokes. Better not to disturb the dead—they had enough trouble with their own spirits, let alone strange ones. Thus they continued on their way, wondering whether the thing that they had seen had come from somewhere else, a world unknown to them. It somehow did not fit into the world which they knew, nor did it fit into the scheme of things with which they could easily cope. It was a bad sign.

They arrived at a settlement up north on the coast called Kilarmitavik, and stayed with relatives. They remained there for a long time. They took part in the hunt, and the hunting was good. Those were carefree days, with an abundance of food. But then Akiviak's father got really sick. The boil on his neck had grown and caused him great pain. He lay moaning on his bunk. They sent for Elijah. He came and started to cut into the boil with his flint knife. By mistake he cut into the artery. Every time they tried to apply pressure on his neck to stop the bleeding, they just about choked him. Thus he bled to death with the family watching helplessly, horror-struck. It was so quiet in the warm dark room that they could hear the dogs moving about outside. The dead man was lying stretched out on the bunk; rays of dim light from the skylight in the ceiling fell upon his face, reflecting a strange brightness from his pale skin. His eyes stared lifelessly into the ceiling, as if he was searching the sky for his own soul.

They sewed him into a blanket of sealskins and covered him with rocks on the burial hill, in the middle of the hillside where there were many other hunters buried before him.

On their way back from the funeral Akiviak noticed that those who had seen his father to the grave walked in zig-zag. They dispersed in all directions, jumped over logs and stones, and made strange motions. This was to mislead the evil spirits which had inflicted bad luck on the dead man, explained his grandfather, to prevent them from doing further damage.

Spring turned into summer. Tigelok took his father's place and became the family's provider.

One day there was a glitter of sun on the rippling surface of the sea, and a gentle breeze. Akiviak was fishing for small prey on the beach. Suddenly he saw a white object moving in from the ocean. This was no iceberg, that he could clearly see. Nor was it an umiak, for it was far too big.

Akiviak dropped his fishing line and ran to the landbrink where a large crowd of Eskimos were gathered. There he was told by the coastal people that what they saw coming in from the sea was a ship which the foreigners used for hunting whale. It resembled the object Akiviak had seen lying on the ice floe on the way north, which had filled everyone with fear.

Akiviak remained on the brink alone while the rest of the crowd ran down to the beach, launched the skin boats, and paddled out to meet the newcomers. They returned with all kinds of articles which they had bartered in exchange for fox skins and baleen. Akiviak had a genuine fear of strangers of any kind. In this case he smelled a curse and kept himself at a safe distance. The fear of witchcraft and supernatural powers from his mountain home remained in him, filled him with unrest, as if he were afraid of falling out with his ancient gods. He thought to himself: Suppose the sea goddess Neqvivik dislikes these foreigners who cause so much disturbance? He had in fact heard Elijah say something to this effect, and he had seen what happened to his father who acted against a taboo.

However, one day Tigelok succeeded in changing Akiviak's mind. Akiviak agreed to go along with Paneak in a skin boat loaded with Eskimos, baleen and fur. They pulled in alongside the ship and climbed aboard. On deck Akiviak saw the largest man he had ever seen. He wore clothing without fur, but had hair of his own on his cheeks, under his nose and on his chin. On his head he wore a black cap with a shiny peak. Men with rolled-up shirtsleeves hurried across the deck. On their arms they had tatoos similar to those the old Eskimo women had on their cheeks. Some of the men had light-colored skin, others were almost black. Akiviak was speechless, and remained standing by the rail. The huge man came towards him, grabbed him by his ear and said something about maktaq. Akiviak was sure that the man said he was dirty like maktaq. He felt a smarting pain in his cheeks as he blushed from embarrassment.

The tall man led the way. Paneak followed him, Akiviak trailing behind. They opened a door, went down some steps and came into a hallway. There Akiviak saw a man with dark golden skin. His hair was curly, like that of a newborn seal, but it was pitch black. His eyes were wilder than those of Elijah at his worst. He was holding the arm of an Eskimo woman, dragging her through a door into another room. She resisted. Akiviak got so mad that he was shaking. He was about to leap to her rescue —he knew the woman—but Paneak held him back. Akiviak was beside himself with rage as he saw the woman forced into the cabin and heard the door locked shut.

Paneak pushed Akiviak into a room where a large wooden slab rested on some logs in the middle of the floor. There were some wooden structures to sit on, and a few sketches on the wall that looked like people. It was here that he lived, this huge man called Captain, and here they bartered. In exchange for a bundle of baleen, Paneak got a mouth organ for Akiviak and a folding knife for Tigelok.

When Akiviak returned home he found his mother seated on the earth floor puffing on a pipe. For this pipe and a pouch of tobacco, she had traded a white fox skin. She filled the pipe with tobacco, ignited a piece of dried moss with her flint lighter, and placed the glowing moss on top of the tobacco in the pipe. Then she started to puff. In order to make the most of her limited supply of tobacco she inhaled deeply and held her breath until she almost fainted. Then she blew out the smoke and coughed.

"What is the good of that?" Akiviak asked himself.

From the foreigners they obtained barrels containing a thick sticky mess, called molasses, and lumps which were called biscuits. They dipped the lumps into the sticky mess and ate them. The taste was rather strange, and they got sticky fingers from it, but this was the way it was supposed to be. In addition, they got hold of some kind of powder called flour and learned how to make doughnuts by dropping lumps of the powder into a stone pot filled with boiling seal oil.

One day Elijah announced that he had to go to Nuvuk, the larger village further north on the coast. Something very interesting was going on there, he said, something he wanted to be a part of. And when he eventually returned from Nuvuk, he wore a black peaked cap similar to the whaling captain's. He called himself "the preacher" and told them about a god he had seen, standing in a basket under the belly of a whale, flying through the air. From high up in the sky, the god had spoken to Elijah and had said, "Go home and cleanse all the women of sin, and make them your followers." Now Elijah ordered all the women to leave their families and come to him. Those who came he washed in ice-cold water until they all had goose pimples. He laid his fat hands upon each of them and felt all their parts, and cleansed them in his own way, a way with which most of the women were quite familiar from previous experience. It therefore puzzled them that anyone could be cleansed by such an act. The ceremony took place in the dark, behind a curtain of caribou skins.

However, the people did believe in Elijah, and all was well until he started to put his hands on those who were clean to begin with, the young unmarried girls. Then even his most ardent followers became doubtful; for this was not at all proper. His career ended when a stranger who called himself a missionary, accompanied by an Eskimo interpreter, arrived from Nuvuk (now known as Point Barrow). They stripped Elijah of all his divinity and dignity and straightened out all those who had gone astray. Elijah was finished. His fellow Eskimos simply gave him the cold shoulder. He ended his days in the mountains, as a Kivitok. There they found him dead, lying in a crevasse.

The end of Elijah, ignominious as it was, brought with it the beginnings of Christianity to the Eskimos. Their meeting with the missionary had aroused the interest of the Utukok people. The legend about the Almighty God appealed to their imagination, and now naturally they all wanted to go to Point Barrow. For along with the new god, there was also a new weapon—the whale gun. By that time the whale had become more than merely meat; it gave them baleen as well, the key to all sorts of new and marvelous inventions: weapons, implements, tools and many other ingenious gadgets. Thus Point Barrow became more and more attractive.

So one day in the fall they set out on their voyage along the coast to the north, Akiviak's family in one skin boat, Paneak's family in another. Every so often they met people going the opposite way, who told fantastic stories about life in Point Barrow. But out at sea they often saw whaling ships adrift, locked in the ice. This was a distressing omen of obstacles ahead.

The wind changed; it blew from the west, pushing the ice towards land, blocking their way to the north. They were unable to proceed any further that year, so they had to settle in for the winter. They collected driftwood, whale ribs and the remains of a wrecked whaling ship, and started to build a house. While the children cut and carried sod for the building site, the adults spent several days digging a deep excavation into the permafrost, starting with a passageway sloping down towards the main room. The skull of a whale was used as a stepping stone into the passage, and the passageway itself was lined with whale ribs to prevent the walls from caving in. The passageway ended under the wooden floor of the main room, which therefore had to be entered through a trapdoor. On either side of this trapdoor, in the main room, there was an oil lamp which provided light and heat. In the far end of the room was a broad plank bench running the full width of the house. This was used both for sitting and for sleeping. The walls and roof were made of banked sod supported by planks. Daylight filtered into the room through the skylight, a wooden frame covered with stretched walrus intestines. Adjacent to this was a smoke hole serving as a vent. The entrance to the house faced inland, away from the sea. This was done so that no light from the house should frighten any animals passing by out at sea. At ground level the entrance to the passageway served as a storm porch and as a shelter for the dogs when the weather was bad. Off from the passageway there were four alcoves, two on either side. The two on the left were used for food storage; the first alcove to the right was called the suuvik, and was used for clothing storage, sleeping, and wife-swapping. The second alcove to the right was the iga, or kitchen, and was used almost exclusively for cooking. It had a fireplace of stones, and a smoke hole in the ceiling. Daylight reached the area through a skylight in the ceiling of the passageway. It was in the iga that the women of the house spent most of their time.

As the days passed, more people arrived from the south. They too built their winter houses, and joined the rest of the dwellers. In the end they had grown into quite a settlement.

One day a group of foreigners appeared. They came from a ship that had been broken down by the pack ice. They needed dogs to make their way south along the coast. Tigelok gave them one of his dogs in exchange for a rifle. Akiviak watched, sitting on the sleeping platform, playing with a string of sinew to while away the time. He was threading his fingers through loops of the string, then stretching out his fingers, trying to make figures resembling bird's feet. Tigelok sat next to him with his new rifle in his lap. Suddenly there was a knock, and up through the trapdoor appeared something resembling the beak of a loon. Akiviak dropped the sinew and crawled into the corner, trembling. The creature climbed up through the door opening. It wore a loon mask over its head, and jumped and shouted. But all it wanted was to invite them all to a drum dance in honor of the foreigners. That evening, they all gathered in the house of the loon-man and danced all night, all except Akiviak. He stayed at home. He could hear the drums in his sleep.

Suddenly he was awakened by a noise; he thought he heard someone moving about in the hallway. He stood up and went out. And there he found one of the foreigners about to harness one of the dogs. Akiviak grabbed the dog and tried to explain that this dog belonged to him. The man pushed him aside, but the boy refused to give in. He struggled and protested the best he could. The man gave him a blow which sent him sprawling on top of the dogs. This caused such a commotion among the animals that the foreigner found it best to get out. But the incident left its traces in Akiviak, for to steal a dog was, in the eyes of an Eskimo, one of the worst things anyone could do. It could even lead to murder. If someone wanted to pick a fight with a man, all he had to do was steal or kill his dog. Then the owner of the dog was obliged to take revenge.

One day when Akiviak was out hunting seals with Tigelok they met a hunter on the sea ice. While they were talking they caught sight of a walrus in the water. They hid behind a large hummock in the screw ice, and the Eskimo hunter started to call like a walrus. He *ugh-ed* with a deep soft voice. Puzzled, the walrus stopped, stretched its neck, and looked around. Then it paddled towards the edge of the ice where the boys were hiding. The hunter called again. The walrus stopped and listened. This time it dug its tusks into the edge of the ice, heaved itself up and came wobbling towards their hiding place. Now it was so close that Akiviak could see distinctly its stiffening guard hairs. The hunter was ready with his spear, but then Tigelok fired. A tremor went through the huge body of the walrus, a stream of blood trickling from its head. Other hunters appeared who had heard the rifle shot, and helped to butcher the animal. Then the women came with the dog teams and hauled the meat ashore. One of the dogs seized the opportunity to steal a piece of skin about as large as the palm of a hand. The greedy beast tried to swallow the piece whole, but the skin got stuck in its throat and the dog choked to death. "That's what happens to one who is too greedy," thought Akiviak to himself.

That spring a foreigner, who called himself John, appeared in the village. He came to whale. He rented two of the Eskimos' whaleboats, engaged crews and hired workers to prepare the catch. He even erected a tent serving as a dining room for all his employees. He appointed a leader for each of the two boats; Paneak became the skipper of one of the boats. Akiviak was hired as one of his crew members. But somehow their luck ran badly, and every time they returned empty-handed John was furious. To make things worse, he never got used to the Eskimos' unpredictable schedule. He demanded a full day's work for a full day's pay, a concept new and strange to the Eskimos. They had no watches, nor did they have any regard for time. They simply carried on as long as they felt like it. They also ate when they felt like it. When one became hungry he put his hand on his stomach, made noises which the women interpreted as signs of hunger, and headed for the dining tent. The women came out and hung large meat pots over the open-air fireplaces. They competed with one another to come first to the men with the meat. It paid off: the one who always came first enjoyed the greatest prestige, like the hunter who regularly was the first to return with his catch.

But when this foreigner John, who was known to be mean, saw them taking their own sweet time, he became so angry that he could hardly control himself. He stormed into the tent, waving his hands about. More than twenty hunters were assembled in the tent. John jumped on the first he could find, and hit him in the face. But then the rest of them leaped to the victim's rescue. They grabbed John, got him down on the floor, piled on top of him, and scratched him vigorously in his face. John cried for help. Finally Akiviak's grandfather heard the row. He hurried to the tent, Akiviak trailing behind him to see what was going on. They found the crowd in the middle of the floor like murderous ants, many against one. The grandfather grabbed the nearest man and lifted him in the air. Then they all dispersed. The old man brought John to his own house so that the poor man could tend to his troubles. He stuck pieces of paper on his wounds to stop the bleeding. In the end it looked as if his face was covered with snowflakes. Everyone laughed, except John. He left the village.

IV

THE PEOPLES
OF THE COAST

As the summer was drawing to an end Akiviak's family set out by skin boat towards Point Barrow. They brought their grandparents with them, as well as Paneak's family, all in one boat. Akiviak's mother was failing. Most of her time she sat quietly in the boat. She mentioned a stepbrother living in Point Barrow; she hoped to see him before it was too late.

They paddled along, day after day, each to an oar.

Finally one day Point Barrow appeared close ahead, a sandspit teeming with people. There were dwellings unlike anything they had ever seen before, in numbers so large that they could not be counted. Two of the houses were very much larger than the rest and were situated by themselves on a hillock. Later on it was learned that one of them was the church, the other was the schoolhouse. And there were summer tents on the beach, an endless row of moulted skin dwellings along the sandspit as far as they could see. The travelers beached the boat and pitched their tent. Akiviak met children of his own age who told him about school, and about someone they called Santa Claus who gave them gifts in the middle of the winter.

By now Akiviak's mother had become so ill that she was unable to stand. She was lying on her sleeping skins, struggling for breath. She had a faraway look in her haunted eyes, her cheeks were flushed with fever. Akiviak who by now was little more than eight summers old kneeled by her side, watching her quietly. When his mother became conscious she took his hand. Her hand burned like a fire. Through the translucent tent skins Akiviak saw the sun rising from the sea, heard the waves pound against the beach. The sunlight flashed like a beacon on the wall of the tent with every wave that rolled in over the sand. Through the open door the sun burned on the water's edge; a brilliant pulsing fire that flared and vanished as the waves rolled in and out. Again and again. He could feel his own pulse beating in rhythm with the sea. Then he noticed that his mother was squeezing his hand gently, as had always been her nature.

"Be good and help the others until we meet again," she said, as if it were only a temporary departure. Akiviak cried silently, tears streaming down his face. He wiped them away with his free hand, dried it on his trousers and strangely, in his grief, noticed that it had become much cleaner than his other hand. All of a sudden the grip on his hand loosened. She was gone.

In the afternoon they buried her. A small and silent procession made its way to the hillside by the tundra. As the mourners left the footpath for the last stretch across the marshes to the graveyard, they met a group of young men who came running down from the tundra. Each of the men carried a wooden stick in his hand and ran as fast as he could. These were runners who had been sent to meet the invited guests from the Colville River, the Nunamiuts, for a messenger feast at Point Barrow. They now returned, racing with the runners from the guest group to see who would be the first to get to the dance house. It was a matter of prestige for the host runners to get back before the guests.

The funeral procession made a brief halt to see who had won. Then they went on. They placed her at the bottom of the burial hill in a bag of skins, and covered her with rocks. Then they walked away. Akiviak remained alone by the grave. Suddenly he heard a cry and saw a shadow move across the grave. A tern shot like an arrow towards the sky, its wings flashing. Akiviak followed it with his eyes until it disappeared. Suddenly his sadness gave way to joy. He was now certain that he had seen his mother's soul released from her suffering body. Light at heart he walked home, eager to share his happiness with his brothers and his sister. But back at the camp he found the tent empty. Apparently everybody was out to watch the messenger festival. He hurried along the rows of empty tents towards the village. He heard voices echoing in the distance, people shouting and dogs barking. Finally, up on a brink, he saw a crowd gathered around a large dance house, a karigi, which apparently had been built for the occasion. As he came nearer he could clearly see a stuffed eagle on top of the roof. He recalled the legend about the eagle, who had brought joy to the people and became the symbol of the messenger festival. This had developed into a most elaborate social event, intended to bring together trading partners from different settlements to barter, exchange gifts, dance, and strengthen bonds of friendship. Akiviak got there in time to witness the meeting between the hosts and their guests from the headwaters of the Colville River. The hosts, the most prominent hunters in Barrow, had taken position in a row in front of the festival house. They were dressed in their finest costumes, with long bearskin mittens on their hands. One of them had an eagle's feather in his hair. Each held a bow in one hand, and an arrow in the other. Behind them stood the messengers who had been sent out to invite the guests, and the runners who had gone to meet the guests when they arrived. Crowds of people filled the open spaces around the festival house and along the foot-paths between the dwellings. In front of the hosts, some distance away, stood the guests, four of five families, surrounded by their runners on top of the brink. It was obvious that they were inland Eskimos, for they were exceptionally tall and their faces were not nearly as broad as those of their coastal cousins.

Then suddenly there was silence. The hosts stirred, lined up side by side and started to move. Slowly they came walking towards the guests, glaring fiercely, as if they were approaching their worst enemies. Suddenly they stopped, lifted their bows and shot their arrows over the heads of the guests, who stood motionless like statues. At the same time the dancers came prancing out of the karigi, behind them the drummer beating his large festival drum. He was banging as hard as he could, but the sound was almost swallowed by the noise and excitement. The dancers performed a ceremonial jump dance in a circle around the guests, then disappeared into the dance house, fol-lowed by the guests and their hosts. Judging from their shouting it appeared that they were exchanging gifts in the house. Then the drums started up again, and the chanting rose and fell with the beat. Now, outside the dance house, gifts were exchanged between the guest runners and all those who had taken part in the preparations for the festival. Finally, the principal host, the umealik, came out and said that now it was enough; there would be no more gifts. The drum dance started again in the karigi, while those outside started to eat of their gifts, sharing what they had, passing out liberal portions of whale meat and maktaq.

It was in the midst of this food distribution that Akiviak found his brother Tigelok. Tigelok, four summers older than Akiviak, had been forward as usual; he could charm his way into anything with his dimples and his sparkling eyes. He had become friendly with Atanga, the daughter of the principal host himself, and had secured a big chunk of meat and a large piece of maktaq, the greater part of which he now gave to Akiviak. But now Tigelok was too busy with Atanga to have any time for his brother. To get rid of Akiviak he persuaded Atanga's little brother to show him the sights of Point Barrow. The two young boys took off together, away from the merrymaking and the drum song which filled the evening air with joy. They walked between sod houses lined up on both sides of the footpath, passing packs of sleeping dogs curled up in the summer grass. Not a human being was to be seen anywhere.

Next to the church stood a square wooden house. Through the window they could see a man who sat staring at a book, joyless and serious. This was the missionary, explained Atanga's brother. Akiviak recognized him; it was the man who had come to Kilamitavik and made an end of Elijah. In a chair next to him sat a stout woman, knitting. She was the missionary's wife, who was also the schoolteacher at Barrow. In a corner of the room a little girl was yawning. She was the missionary's daughter.

"Sh-sh," whispered the boy. "They are not to be disturbed, they are observing their day of rest."

Further down the path they came upon a log cabin with lighted windows. Inside were readymade weapons hanging on the wall, equipment and supplies of all kinds, for the most part implements which Akiviak had never before seen or heard of. This was the store, he was told. Behind a counter a lean fellow bustled back and forth arranging things on the shelves, piling up packages and sorting out goods. In the room behind the store, through an open door, they saw a heavy-set man with a moustache bent over an account book, looking dissatisfied.

"He is rich," said the boy, with a respectful voice. "He is the owner of ten whaleboats, and many men work for him." Akiviak wondered how it was possible to look so dissatisfied surrounded by all this wealth.

When the boys returned to the festival there was still a large crowd of people assembled outside the dance house. They appeared to be in high spirits, and judging from the noise inside the tent the dancers were in a state of wild excitement. Akiviak peeped through the door. It was fairly dark and quite warm. People were stepping about, breathing heavily in their thick parkas, waving their arms, twisting and turning with the rhythm of the drums. Men and women danced together. Hosts and guests took turns occupying the floor, a furry mass moving about on soft skin boots, filled with a lust for life and all its possibilities. A song leader sang first, one verse at a time; then all joined in the refrain, with a roar that echoed over the fields and marshes. The drummers were sitting in a row on the floor, their eyes tightly closed, the knuckles of their hands white and the perspiration pouring down their foreheads. Their rhythm was so infectious that even Akiviak, who was only looking on, was carried away by its magic. He could feel in the masses around him a vibration, a joyful intoxication that was almost uncontrollable. Those who did not sing stood and grinned, faces beaming in the dusk. Akiviak felt happy for his people; he felt safe being one of them, proud of his origin. He felt an urge to mix with his kinsfolk, to communicate with them. But most of those of his own age had already sneaked away to seek their other, more intimate pleasures, to explore the wonders of nature in their own natural ways, in the open, in the grass between the gravel mounds, in the shelter of the meat racks, under the skin boats on the moonlit beach.

Elated, Akiviak went to bed alone and fell asleep among his caribou skins.

The climax came on the third day of the festival, when the guests were asked to stay outside while the hosts carried their gifts into the dance house. Akiviak seized the opportunity to take a look through the door, and there he saw a heap of treasures on the floor in front of the drums. There were sealskins, skin bags filled with whale blubber and seal oil, spears, arrows and bows, maktaq, parkas and mukluks, even a brand-new sled.

Surely those who could afford such costly gifts had to be rich. He knew, of course, that traditionally the burden of giving lay with the hosts; the guests always received much more than they were obliged to give.

Then the guests were escorted into the tent. They were summoned by name, one by one. The drummer gave a few thundering bangs on the drum as each guest stepped forward to receive his gift. Then followed the ceremonial jump dance in a slow tempo, in thanksgiving to the generous hosts.

On the fourth day they all gathered on the field in front of the dance house, split up into two groups and started to kick a large skin ball about. In the confusion it was impossible to see who had won. Next there was a foot race in which everyone could participate, running from one end of the field to the other. Tigelok came first, winning by a great margin. Instantaneously the boy from the mountains became a person of importance.

While the game was in full swing and the spirit was at its peak one of the guests suddenly stood up in the middle of the field, raised his arms, and shouted:

"Next time it is our turn. Then you come to us!"

This turned out to be a signal for everyone to return to the karigi for the departing dance. Everyone assembled outside and waited. Suddenly two figures appeared, carrying bows and arrows and wearing eagle masks on their heads. They danced in a squatting position, moved in a circle around the hosts and amongst the crowd. All of a sudden they shot their arrows over the heads of the hosts, giving the sign that the festival had come to an end. The guests took off for their boats, followed by the hosts, and trailed by the rest of the crowd. The spectators gathered on the shore, watching as their guests boarded their skin boats shoved off and rowed away, back to the headwaters of the Colville.

The crowd dispersed, everyone returning to his own ordinary

lot, Akiviak to his bitter bereavement. It was bad enough to have lost his mother; even worse was that the family had to be broken up. Not that Tigelok was unable to provide for his brothers and sister. The problem was that Akiviak's sister Sila was not old enough to look after their younger brother, Kanayuk, who was therefore brought to their uncle Paneak, their mother's brother. Akiviak went to live with his mother's stepbrother, Kopak. Sila got a job as a maid for the schoolteacher and moved into the missionary's house. Tigelok went to the umealik, Apayaok, as a member of his boat crew, and as a prospective son-in-law.

Now Akiviak could go to school. Alone, he arrived at the large white building with its glass windows and climbed the three steps leading up to the wide double door. He barely had the courage to go through with it. Cautiously he looked through the half-open door. Inside he could see the class assembled, Eskimo children of all ages. They stared curiously at him, some of the children whispered, others giggled. Akiviak tiptoed on his worn sealskin mukluks across the floor, which creaked under his feet. He sat down at the edge of a long bench in the back of the classroom. Now he felt safer and could better look around. Behind him in a corner stood a large wood-burning iron stove. Facing the class, there was a blackboard which covered most of the wall. And there, in front of the blackboard, seated at a table on a platform, was the teacher, the stout wife of the missionary, her hair rolled into a ball on the top of her head. There was a stern look on her ruddy face as she rapped her knuckles on the table.

"Silence!"

Then she started to read the names of the pupils from a list, one by one. She squinted over her glasses, waiting for the pupil in question to raise his hand and say "Here." But when it was Akiviak's turn, it came so unexpectedly that he, in his confusion, simply got up and remained standing, stiff like a statue, unable to utter a word. The rest of the class started to laugh. Akiviak could feel the blood rising to his head, and his heart pounded in his chest. Then he was called forward to answer questions as to who he was, and where he came from. Then he had to step up on the platform in front of the blackboard to learn how to draw letters with a piece of chalk, the whole alphabet from beginning to end, while the rest of the class pronounced the letters in chorus. It took time, but he did get through. He soon became familiar with the new words, and what they meant. He was issued a whole new pencil, many times the length of the small piece of pencil he had received as a present from his brother. He was given a notebook to write in, and a picture book to look at.

After school one day Akiviak went down to the drying rack on the brink to bring home a chunk of meat. There he happened to meet the missionary's daughter. She was more talkative and friendlier than usual; it appeared that she had something on her mind. Finally she found an excuse to get Akiviak under a skin boat which lay upside down on the beach. There he discovered that she was merely inquisitive; she wanted to know what he looked like in the nude, as if she had never seen a nude boy before. That is funny, thought Akiviak, who was used to being nude among nude people when he went to sleep every night, or when it was too hot in the house to wear clothing. This exhibition therefore was of little interest to him. Instead, he hurried home to his books, and left the girl sitting there alone with her curiosity.

As the days passed, a new world was opened to him at the school. The more he learned, the more curious he became. Finally, his thirst for knowledge occupied him completely. While the rest of the children were out playing in the evenings, he stayed inside working on his problems, laboring over his books. He sat on the platform in Kopak's peat house, doing his arithmetic by the light of a stone lamp. The old man, Kopak, was sitting on the floor, his legs stretched out in front of him, carving the handle of a harpoon, looking sceptically at the boy and his doings. Kopak's wife was squatting in front of the stove, occupied with her cooking. Akiviak, pale and serious, was completely absorbed in his work, leaving marks on the pages from his greasy fingers as he thumbed through his book. Every so often he felt he had to communicate with his foster parents, to share his discoveries with them. He related to them everything he came across about the earth and the sky, about the sun and the moon, about all that existed in the strange world south of the mountains which was many times greater than the world they knew.

"Ai," said Kopak, not quite sure what to believe.

Akiviak learned quickly. Soon he was the most brilliant student in the school. Not only was his memory good, but he also had a rare ability to come up with original ideas and solutions. He had a most vivid imagination, which occasionally was apt to run away with him. And he was a gifted speaker. People always listened to what he had to say, even though they might not agree with it all, for his voice had a warmth to it that was unique. Even in his ability to master the white man's language he was outstanding. Thus he grew and became mature exceptionally early, and wherever he appeared he was recognized.

His stepfather, Kopak, looked at him: "Akiviak can dream with one eye and see with the other!"

In school he was taught arithmetic, an art previously unknown to his people. But the teacher conducted the course at the practical level, aiming at the problems of everyday life. One day she said to Akiviak: "Suppose you are going to sell baleen to the trader, and suppose he pays you five pounds of flour for each pound. How much flour should he give you for 100 pounds of baleen?"

Akiviak started to figure, and thought of the amount of flour they had received in exchange for their whalebones. It gradually dawned on him that the trader must have cheated them. But the teacher was merely using a hypothetical example; Akiviak misunderstood and took the quoted prices seriously. This led to a serious conflict.

Akiviak shared his discovery with Kopak. Kopak related it further to his friends. Soon everybody knew about the "swindle." Finally it reached the ear of Peter, the trader. He began to hate Akiviak, who had turned his customers against him. Naturally, Akiviak noticed the hostile attitude of the trader, sensitive as he was, but actually he felt a bit proud at having been so clever.

Then, one evening, when Akiviak was in the store, the old hunter Apayaok came in. He needed some implements, a little tea and a bag of biscuits. Like the rest of them he charged his purchases to his account, with the understanding that he would pay his debt with the game and fur he brought in later. The value of his goods would be set according to the going price at the time of the settlement; or subject to the estimate of the trader. But the trader transferred the value of the purchased items into cash dollars, listed the items neatly in a column in his ledger, and started to add the figures. Akiviak was checking the trader's additions and discovered a mistake. The error amounted to several dollars in Apayaok's favor. Thus it was not a matter of cheating, just poor arithmetic.

Akiviak could not help it. He said as carefully as he could that the trader had made an error. At this Peter lost his temper. He took exception to being corrected by a puppy, and an Eskimo puppy at that! He became so mad that he hit the boy and shouted angrily, "Shut up, you lazy kid! Get out and hunt like the others, instead of hanging around here stirring up trouble."

An unpleasant atmosphere developed in the store. The Eskimos withdrew and quietly went their way, for hostility was not to their liking and quarrels were alien to their nature. Besides, Akiviak could expect protection only from his next of kin, his stepfather Kopak, who was not present.

Akiviak, however, was not about to yield. He knew that he was in the right. He pointed to the book, added the figures and proved, that an error is an error. And when at last it dawned on the trader that the error represented a loss to himself, the matter suddenly seemed quite different. The tone of his voice turned quite gentle, almost fatherly. It slowly occurred to him that he might possibly make use of the boy, dependable and eager as he was.

"Let this now be a lesson to you, my lad," he said to Akiviak. Then he put a small bag of candy in the boy's hand as a token of his generosity.

A few days later Akiviak was hired as a part-time helper, working in the evenings. He emptied the toilet buckets, cleared up the storeroom, sorted out various bills and pieces of paper and added columns of figures. He was given some sugar, tea and a little flour as payment when he went home at night. But Akiviak had taken note of the incident at the store that evening. He had gained a valuable insight into the nature of the white man. Gradually it became increasingly clear to him that he must protect his people against injustice. He resolved to learn the white man's language, and his way of dealing with figures.

That year a new foreigner, a trader, appeared in Point Barrow. Now there were two traders in the place who quarrelled and competed with one another, and fought over their Eskimo customers. This caused a price war which some of the Eskimos were smart enough to use to their advantage. Peter was still the more prominent and prosperous of the two, with less than ten whaleboats in operation. The new trader had only three. It was obvious that they could not stand each other. They tried to encourage discord among the Eskimos and slandered each other whenever the occasion presented itself. And in turn these two traders made derogatory remarks about the white whalers who were their common competitors, who bought baleen and fur directly from the Eskimo hunters, at prices which often were higher than they themselves were willing to pay. Every time the traders quarreled the Eskimos withdrew. They avoided taking any sides, preferring to remain on good terms with both of them for safety's sake. All this Akiviak observed from his vantage point as errand boy at the store. He despised the behavior of the white men, but at the same time he himself was in their service. Thus, Peter the trader had cleverly neutralized his effectiveness as a troublemaker by making him his servant. Akiviak swallowed his frustration until things cooled down and the tension had eased a bit.

Akiviak was, by now, 14 summers old and mature enough to serve as a full member of the whaling crew. He became the youngest man on Kopak's boat. At Point Barrow whaling was considered a basis for life, an essential foundation for existence. A whole culture was built around whaling, a culture based on a mixture of superstition and tradition with roots extending far back to ancient times. Specific rituals and religious offerings were held at certain times, all according to the moon. These events came in a fixed sequence, from the fall to the start of the first whaling season in the spring.

The skin boat ceremony took place in late autumn, with offerings to the gods in gratitude for granting good luck in the hunt. Their larders were filled. In meat cellars deep in the permafrost, they had stored frozen seal carcasses, whale meat and blubber, fish, plants and berries. Hanging on the drying racks there were both fish and meat, harvests from the sea and the land.

On a stretched walrus skin at the very top of the drying rack, well out of reach of the hungry dogs, the Eskimos had carefully placed their sealskin pokes filled with blubber, maktaq and berries which the sun in the course of the summer months had melted into a mash. This was then stored for a second year, together with walrus heads and whale flippers, maturing, to be used as offering and ceremonial food on special occasions.

The ceremony started when Kopak got up at dawn, turned his face to the west, and remained standing in this position while he put on his sealskin trousers. While so doing he muttered a series of words in which the word Agvok, meaning whale, occurred at fairly regular intervals. It was a prayer to the goddess of the game, Neqvivik, which had been handed down from father to son for generations:

"Gladly you gave us the gifts of the sea, this year again like the year before, gentle Neqvivik; give us the gales from the south, for in easterly winds the sea is void of whale, O Goddess Neqvivik!"

Akiviak did as his master. He knew that this was the day, for now the crew had refurbished the skin boat, the umiak. They had stretched a new walrus hide over the wooden boat frame, using a female walrus hide split in two, carefully fitted over the frame, and sewn together with tiny stitches of sinew pulled through tallow and threaded through the hide with a bone needle.

Akiviak followed Kopak out of the house. There the rest of the crew were waiting, standing around the boat. Among them was the brother of Kopak, and his son Konuku. Silently they lifted the boat, carried it on their shoulders to the beach, circled the boat rack and put the umiak down in the sand. Kopak took the steering oar and placed it on the ground in front of the bow, the blade pointing towards the sea. And now Kopak's wife appeared. She stepped out of the house in a sun-bleached over-parka made from the intestines of a bearded seal. She carried a bowl carved out of a log of driftwood. The crew took their places alongside the boat facing the sea; Kopak in the rear. Akiviak heard the woman's steps in the gravel as she slowly walked under the boat rack and around the steering oar. She stopped in front of Akiviak, turned towards the sea, and lifted the bowl filled with finely cut pieces of seal meat and caribou tallow. Then she bent forward into the boat so that she almost pushed Akiviak over with her buttocks, and placed the bowl carefully in front of the middle seat. Then she returned the same route she came.

Kopak went forward, bent down and filled his hand with meat from the bowl and tossed the food like a rain of crumbs over the boat. Three times he repeated this act. Then he sprinkled three handfuls of ceremonial food over the sea. He turned around and threw three more handfuls of food onto the boat rack, turned to the south and tossed three portions of food towards the tundra, as a favor to the spirits of the dead hunters. Each time, he mumbled his offering prayer to the game goddess Neqvivik, with a voice so quiet that it could barely be heard:

"If you will take my humble tallow I shall serve you well and worship you willingly, gracious Goddess Neqvivik. And you, Agvok, I am here to honor you. Lend me your luck, grant me gladly your fat. Give me meat to fill my belly. Be generous, Agvok."

Then he smeared a handful of food on the bow of the boat, where his small skin bag filled with amulets and charms would hang during whaling. Finally, he smeared some food on the rack. When this was done, all members of the crew were allowed to help themselves three times from the food bowl. They picked up the food carefully with their fingers, which they licked afterwards. They lifted the boat back onto the rack and tied it bottom up. Kopak put the oar back in place. Then they walked away.

The harpoon rope ceremony followed a few days later. Kopak had been up early that morning and had brought out the long walrus-skin rope, which fastened the harpoon head to the seal-skin floats when whaling. He had stretched it out high above the ground between poles stationed from the house all the way down to the boat rack and on to the sea.

In the morning people began to gather between the houses. Now they assembled under the rope. At a signal from Kopak, they all started to run. They raced along the beach, then on the footpath across the fields, up the gentle slope leading to the burial hill, around the tall rock up on the summit, and back again. The youngsters ran as fast as they could. The older people trotted more cautiously after them, and turned around when the youngsters came back on the return leg. The bowlegged Akiviak ran with ease, barely moving his arms. He knew that much was at stake in this foot race. He pushed on and ran for all he was worth. Out in the open field he got a stitch in his side, but he forced himself on without slackening his speed, exerting himself until he almost blacked out. When he reached the burial hill Konuku was ahead of him. The rest of the contestants followed, breathing heavily. Then Akiviak noticed that Konuku's legs had begun to stiffen in the last stretch of the incline, and that he had slowed down. Akiviak gained on him. By now the stitch had gone, he started to breath easier, and as the runners rounded the rock on their way back, Akiviak was in the lead, trailed by Konuku a few paces behind. But then Akiviak felt his own legs begin to stiffen. It was difficult for him to bring them forward; he was about to stumble. He tried to change his pace, shortening his stride. It helped. Instead of running on the gravel on the footpath, he chose to stay on the grass where the ground was firmer, and therefore easier to run on. When he had run so far that he could see the houses and all the women gathered ahead of him, he got his second wind. He sprinted all the way to the finish and fell flat on his face at the women's feet.

This was the first time that Akiviak had excelled himself physically. By winning that foot race he had, according to custom, won the right to serve as harpooner on the whaleboat. As a token of his distinction, the harpooner's cap was placed on his head. This was a large cap made of caribou fur, with a tuft of long caribou hair on top.

Then the offerings started. Kopak rounded up his crew. His wife came out of the house, clad in her fanciest parka. She carried a wooden tray filled with chopped whale maktaq. She placed the tray on the ground while the spectators kept the dogs away with long wooden poles. Then Kopak carried the tray down to the boat. The rest of the crew followed him, then the crowd. And there Kopak made offerings and threw the food about, mumbled and whispered his prayers to the spirits, closely guarded secrets which none except his own crew were permitted to hear. When this was done, they sat down on a log of driftwood and ate the rest of the food.

V

THE HUNTING
OF WHALES

"It is the early training that makes a whaler of a man," Kopak said one evening as he was talking to his fellow hunters, as was their custom. They would spend long evenings telling whaling legends, and tales of their failures and successes. Theirs was a language of pictures and symbols, and their accounts were filled with instructive details about the art of whaling which the young Akiviak absorbed with keen interest. This was their form of instruction, aimed at teaching the young mind to think like the whale, to become familiar with its ways, so that the young hunter in a given situation would act automatically. He had to prepare himself mentally, condition his will power and synchronize his reactions with those of the others in the crew, so that they all could act together as a unified team. It was the function of the ceremonies to create this unity, and for this reason Akiviak had to take part in the different whaling rituals.

In this traditional way Akiviak had joined the most exciting of all Eskimo ventures: the hunting of whales. A new chapter of his life had begun. By virtue of his performance he had become an important member of the crew. Now he had to use his time during the winter in preparation for the spring whaling. He had to master every aspect of the art, above all the skill of throwing the harpoon. Soon he was able to hit a seagull in the head with a stone at a distance five times the length of a whale-boat, and to kill an owl with a single throw. He had to be that accurate. He soon became one of the most skillful harpooners, with remarkable power in his strike. He discovered that by using a special throwing stick he could throw his harpoon five times farther than before. He tested his marksmanship by throwing his harpoon at an old seal poke from a distance of twenty paces. Of one hundred and fifty throws, he failed merely three times.

And so the winter passed. Akiviak went out with Kopak hunting seals and white foxes; he carried ice for drinking water, and he attended to the equipment and hunting gear. Occasionally he went to school, but this was rather irregular since there was a shortage of fuel for heating the schoolhouse. In between he helped in the store.

When spring came they started to prepare for the moon festival, the main offering before the commencement of the whaling season. It began one morning at the new moon, when Kopak asked Akiviak to put on his new sealskin mittens and climb up on the meat rack to fetch down the food offering. They were not allowed to touch this food with their bare hands or with mittens which had been used previously for hunting, since this would be an offense to the spirit of the whale.

Akiviak brought down the sealskin bags filled with a mixture of dried meat, blackberries and seal oil. He brought down the winddried head of a walrus, a bundle of dried cod and a walrus gall bladder filled with caribou tallow. Kopak, standing on the ground below with ceremonial mittens on his hands, collected it all with great care and tied it on his sled into the skin of a bearded seal. He then brought it home, where it was stored in his hallway and left to thaw until the full moon.

Then early one morning Akiviak was awakened by the unfamiliar sound of someone singing. He raised his head, and in the pale moonlight streaming in from the smoke hole he saw a face, tanned and wrinkled, the features strained, the eyes tightly closed, the lips barely moving. It was Kopak squatting on the floor, softly chanting his worship to the gods, swaying as he sang his monotonous song. In the strange mixture of pale moonlight and flame from the oil lamp Kopak's dark face glowed a golden brown. The rest of his body was scarcely traceable in the half-light which gradually faded into complete darkness. Now Kopak chanted, chopping meat on a wooden tray with sealskin mittens on his hands. The food offering lay scattered on the earthen floor around the centerpost of the hut, from which hung the weather-bleached steering oar and the whaling harpoon. A seal poke used for whaling was suspended from the ceiling. Something moved in a corner, stirring in the dark. It was Kopak's wife. Soon she appeared in the moonbeam, dressed in a white anorak, a sweater-like hooded jacket made of walrus intestines; she wore mittens on her hands. She squatted over the oil lamp and mixed melted blubber oil with crowberries and juice from the sealskin bag.

When Kopak and his wife were finished they covered the food with a sealskin. Then the woman brought in the walrus gall bladder filled with caribou tallow. She placed the bladder on the sealskin and started to undress, taking off one garment after the other, until she stood naked on the floor. This she had to do in order to approach the whale spirit free of any garment which had been contaminated by contact with other animals. Then she put on her mittens and rolled out the tallow. She mixed it with warm blubber oil in a wooden tray, making a dough which she whipped with a wooden stick until it resembled the brain of an animal. This was cut into small lumps which she rolled out into round balls and carefully placed in a wooden bowl. Finally she put the bowl on the floor and covered it with a sealskin. Kopak was still chanting. Then he stopped. Both of them remained silent for a while, then asked Akiviak to rise. When the rest of the crew arrived the woman put on her ceremonial clothes, attached a wisp of caribou hair to her braid, and went out with the bowl of tallow balls. The crew followed her, each man carrying a bowl of food offering. The moon was fading. Like a ghost the woman moved with a slow gait alone to the beach. She went under the boat rack, placed the bowl in the skin boat, and returned to the house. Then came the crew, but they followed a different route, avoiding the woman. One by one they walked up to the skin boat, and put the food bowls carefully down under the seats. Then they lifted the boat and carried it to the sea, boarded it and rowed a short distance. There they pulled in the oars and let the boat drift with the current until the sun appeared above the crest of the mountain.

The snow-covered tundra sparkled in the morning light. Drifting ice rose and fell as in a mirage on the horizon. The rising sun tinted the skin cover of the boat blood red. Kopak placed his steering oar in the bow of the umiak, mumbled a ceremonial verse, tossed a ball of tallow into the air in front of the boat; it landed with a splash in the water. He threw another ball to portside, and one to starboard. Finally, he sprinkled a handful of chopped meat into the water behind the boat. Then he sat and they rowed back to the shore, where they were greeted by a flock of relatives. Together they consumed the rest of the food offering, and then secured the boat back onto the boat rack. Then Kopak said:

"Now, we think whale!"

The old men kept a constant watch on the coastline. They stood in the chilling wind, shivering in their yellowish-white windbreakers. They rubbed their hands inside their parkas and spat.

One day the message came from the shore: they had seen whales. Akiviak wanted to know if they would go out at once, but the only reply he got out of Kopak was a vague "maybe" ("nara"), for as everyone knew such matters were decided by the elders on the brink. They had to make up their own minds first, then ask the spirits for advice and see what indications they got from their amulets. It also depended on the arrival of the migratory birds, which had not yet occurred, and on the phase of the moon, which was now on the decline. Furthermore, the whales seemed rather restless now, and were blowing in all directions. All in all, concluded the elders, the situation was not good. It was evident that the old men would have the last word. It was tough to be young and eager among so many oldsters who had so much to say.

But then came the word, finally! The day was sunny and calm; loose ice drifted on the fjord. There was a strange feeling of anticipation in the air. Messengers were sent to summon the whaling crews. In almost every house men were getting ready. People were rushing about everywhere, boats were being loaded, crew members were arranging tackle and gear, dogs howled. Akiviak had never felt so much excitement before.

On the beach Akiviak ran into his brother Tigelok. He was a member of Apayaok's crew, in a wooden whaleboat belonging to the trader. Tigelok told him that someone had knocked a hole in the bottom of their wooden boat; one of the older men, he guessed, who believed that the wooden boat would scare the whale away, and for this reason would rather see it sunk. And besides, the crew of the wooden whaleboat were Christians and had not made their offerings to the ancient gods; little wonder that they were being punished!

Akiviak glanced at Apayaok suspiciously. Apayaok was thrashing around like a bear, spitting tobacco juice. To be sure of his own safety Akiviak checked the amulet bag hanging around his neck. Then he ran over to join his crew.

They put out the boat and shoved off, paddling as hard as they could. Several other umiaks could be seen in the open leads between the ice floes. It was a race to be the first to reach the whales. A large ice floe blocked their way, so they climbed up on the ice to take a look. The whales were nowhere to be seen. Kopak said that most probably they were sunning themselves on the surface in this lovely weather.

They decided to wait. Pulling the boat up onto the ice, they put wooden blocks under the keel so it wouldn't freeze to the ice. Then they rolled out their sleeping skins and settled down. They ate their meat raw, for they were not permitted to make any fire: it was an old tradition that, while whaling, no one should eat boiled meat until the arrival of the first migratory birds. They slept in watches, half of the crew sleeping while the other half was on the lookout.

It was evening, the sun low over the horizon shedding a golden glow on the ice. The floes were reflected in the mirror-like sea. Akiviak was on the lookout, standing next to Kopak on a large hummock, scanning the horizon. Suddenly something caught his eye. In the distance, where the sea and the sky fused into a single shimmering band against the fading light of the setting sun, a spout of water arched into the air. Akiviak jumped. His first reaction was to call the rest of the crew, but he restrained himself, for he had been told that his shouting might disturb the whale, sensitive as it was to any sound. He was not even supposed to point, for to point at a whale, in the Eskimo way of thinking, was the same as to insult its soul. So he nodded his head toward the horizon, stared at Kopak and whispered "Agvok," so softly that he could barely be heard. Kopak merely blinked his eyes under his fur-rimmed parka hood; he had seen it all before. Akiviak could hardly control his eagerness. Shaking, without a word, he woke up those who were sleeping. They carried the boat back to sea and paddled in the direction of the whale blow, Akiviak in front at his oar. He looked back at Kopak, who was steering. Motionless, Kopak peered ahead, his eyes fixed on a distant object ahead, his face a mask void of any emotion. Now they paddled full speed, and the sea foamed around the bow of the boat. Akiviak pulled on his oar until his fingers were blue. All the time his eyes never left the horizon ahead; he saw the blow at fairly regular intervals as the whale surfaced to breathe, shooting a geyser of water high into the air. By now he thought he could see the animal's back emerge from the water; they were getting closer. Akiviak became impatient. What were they waiting for? He turned around for a quick look at Kopak. But Kopak, cool as ever, cleared his throat and said softly: "Get ready now, Akiviak."

Quickly and quietly Akiviak pulled in his oar, grabbed the harpoon, and took his position in the front of the boat. The skin rope attached to the harpoon head lay neatly coiled behind him. He quivered like the leaves of a willow. Now there were several whaleboats in the water. Akiviak tried to make himself as inconspicuous as he could, knowing full well that he was no more than a beginner. But the excitement soon made him forget his embarrassment. He regained his balance and was once more the instinctive hunter.

By now it appeared as if there was a whole school of whales in the vicinity, but Kopak was pursuing the one they had observed first. It was playing in the water, blowing at short intervals, gliding close to the surface like a dark shadow, shattering the mirrorlike surface of the sea every time it broke through the water to breathe. Now Kopak changed course in order to intercept his prey. Akiviak was ready, holding the harpoon in his right hand, slightly raised, the harpoon head securely pressed into the pin at the end of the handle.

The men paddled, their eyes fixed on the surface of the sea. Then it happened. Just ahead to starboard the whale rose like a submerged island out of the sea, looked balefully at them with one eye, blew, and slid back into the sea again. Akiviak froze into a standing statue, completely paralyzed by the sight of the huge monster in the sea. He hesitated merely for a moment, but it felt like an eternity. And when at long last he recovered his senses and threw his harpoon after the animal it was too late.

The blade of the harpoon head failed to penetrate the whale's thick skin, and was left floating on the sea. Ashamed, Akiviak retrieved his rope and pulled the harpoon back into the boat. The rest of the crew did not say a word, but Akiviak could feel what they were thinking. He took a quick look at Kopak. The skipper was undisturbed by the failure; he kept about his business as if nothing had happened. As far as Akiviak was concerned it made no difference anyhow, for according to tradition the harpooner could only throw his weapon once at the same whale. It was an ancient agreement between man and whale to the effect that the whale should also have a sporting chance. They had to show sufficient respect for the whale, and were not to tease it or poke at it with the harpoon. If they hit it, they were to hit it properly or else they were to leave it alone.

Kopak had shifted his attention to another whale blowing further out. It moved slowly in the water. The waves rippled gently against the boat, curved columns of water on both sides of the bow. Kopak held the steering oar firmly in his hand. He appeared sure of himself; as if by instinct, he guided the boat to the spot where the whale would come up for its next blow. Akiviak, standing in the bow, was peering ahead, so tense that it hurt. Then he looked down and saw the head of a whale emerge underneath the bow of the boat. Suddenly it felt as if the boat was being lifted into the air. This sudden motion caused Akiviak to lose his balance; he fell towards the starboard side of the boat. As he fell he grasped the harpoon handle firmly with both hands and thrust the point into the back of the whale just at the depression between head and body. Putting all his weight on the shaft he drove it down as hard as he could. For a terrible moment he found himself looking into the whale's eye. And then the hard flesh suddenly gave way and the harpoon plunged home. In the nick of time Akiviak let go of the harpoon, for now the huge body came brushing along the side of the boat. Quickly and without a word the two forward men pulled in their oars and

threw the floats overboard. Suddenly the huge animal leaped out
of the water and half of its body rose like a mountain out of the
sea. Then it blew, and a spray of red foam rained down on the
boat. It dived with a splash so violent that it almost toppled the
boat. The rope shot out over the gunwale.

The whale dived almost straight down, pulling the floats
under as if they were nothing but a couple of corks. The whale
soon surfaced again, dived, reappeared and dived anew. When
it came up again it was obviously in trouble, and from now on
the interval between each ascent became shorter. Kopak and his
crew stayed behind it and watched the floats, but kept a safe
distance between the whale and the boat. Then Kopak changed
his course, and told the men to row as fast as they could. When
the whale surfaced again, it came just alongside the boat, less
than an oar's length away. Calmly the men pulled in their oars,
grabbed the long whale lances and thrust them deep into the
animal's side. It dived, but came to the surface almost at once.
Soon it stopped moving, turned over and lay floating on its back
on the surface of a crimson sea. Kopak planted the pole bearing
his sign in the whale, to mark that the catch belonged to him.
He then untied the bag of amulets from the bow and touched
the whale with it. As Kopak opened the bag Akiviak could see
that it contained a small stone shaped like a whale, a dried lens
from a whale's eye, and two long bird beaks. These beaks Kopak
now brought out, tied one of them to his own head, and the
other to Akiviak's. Then they rowed in a circle around the whale
while Kopak shouted the traditional whale cry: "Vo-ho-ho-hov!"
By now more whaleboats had arrived. They fastened another
harpoon to the lip of the whale, to which they tied the necessary towlines, and soon a whole convoy of skin boats was
towing the whale to the edge of the shore ice. As they approached the shore, Kopak resumed his vo-ho-ing. It rang out
over the sea, like the harsh cry of an animal. Many people had
gathered on the beach to greet the whale. In front of them all
was Kopak's wife, carrying a wooden bowl filled with a mixture

of sour plants and water. She wore her sunbleached ceremonial parka and a tuft of caribou hair in her braids. As the boat hit the sand Kopak stood up in the stern, his steering oar raised in the air. Akiviak with his harpoon stood in the bow of the boat. The rest of the crew remained seated, resting their oars in the water. On a signal from Kopak they started to rock the boat. The woman on the beach swayed in time to the movements of the craft. Then they stopped and all was quiet. Kopak lifted his oar and turned his face to the north. His wife turned the same way, and lifted her wooden bowl above her head. While standing in this position Kopak again shouted the whale cry. Then he and his wife turned to the south and repeated the same act. When this was done the woman handed her wooden bowl to Akiviak, who didn't drink but passed it along to Kopak, who drank from it, then passed it on to the nearest man, until the whole crew had had a drink from the bowl. Lastly, it was Akiviak's turn. He took a mouthful of the sour liquid and gave the bowl back to Kopak's wife, who was still standing on the beach, her legs spread wide apart. Akiviak then concluded the ceremony by forcefully throwing his harpoon into the sand, between the woman's legs. Then they all took hold of the towlines, pulled the whale up on the beach and started to cut it apart. They shared the meat and the blubber in accordance with their ancient rules, among the crews and the rest of the people of the village. The children had their hands full keeping the dogs away. When the chores were done an old woman was called upon to tattoo the whale sign on Akiviak's right arm. Kopak painted another whale on his steering oar, with a mixture of soot from the oil lamp and fluid from the anterior chamber of the whale's eye.

They caught no more whales that spring. But for the bones and part of the blubber of the one whale which they did get, Kopak bought himself a brand new whale gun, a harpoon gun (also called a darting gun), and lances with blades of iron. He started to prepare himself for the fall hunt.

The summer was spent waiting for the whales to appear.

These were idle, carefree, endless days, for the nights were as bright as the days. When the cod appeared in the lagoon they went there to fish. And when the time came for the salmon to run up the river, they went there to help themselves. In between they caught birds, collected eggs and helped the women gather plants and berries on the tundra. There were sunny days with passing clouds and gentle breezes, days when it rained and the chilly wind blew in from the south, days with the fog rolling in from the Arctic Ocean with the west wind.

A typical fall day on the Chukchi seacoast at Point Barrow, the air clear, the sky sunny without a cloud. The ice floes were adrift on the sea, sparkling in the sun. The Arctic mirage on the horizon created an endless succession of transient miracles: icy structures rising into fantastic castles and towers that soon sank into the sea, only to give way to new creations no less magnificent. On the shore a group of young boys was throwing stones at a flock of ducks that rested on the sea, riding the undertow, in and out, searching for prey. A little further up the beach little girls in their colorful fur parkas played in the brilliant sand. The gentle breeze carried with it the smell of the wild vegetation of the tundra. It sighed like a breath down across the niggerheads and marshes, stirred the grass on the burial hill, passed the church and the summer tents and peat-covered sod houses, passed the schoolhouse and the boat racks on the beach. The sounds of life rang through the village, happy voices of playing children, a chorus of howling dogs, squawking seagulls quarreling with the terns over a dead seal, squealing Eskimo children with owl feathers in their hair and wooden sticks for pistols. Between the sod houses the women were hanging out their wash to dry, laughing and gossiping. Peter, the trader, a fellow with a large moustache and a fat belly, lurked somewhere in the background with a pair of binoculars around his neck, keeping an eye on them all while the hunters prepared for the whaling.

Then came the time when the whales passed by on their

annual migration to the west. The first sign of this event was the appearance of the large whaling ships. They came from the east, slowly drifting out on the horizon. They moved without sail, trailing a long stream of smoke. The villagers, awed by the smoke, flocked to the beach and said that this was surely a miracle. Akiviak then explained that these were vessels powered by steam, and that they only used sails in an emergency. They burned coal, hence the black smoke. The ships kept cruising back and forth in the distance, but apparently had not as yet lowered any of the whaleboats, which meant that the hunt had not started. The old men on the beach were waving their arms about and shaking their heads, but agreed on one thing: by all indications it was too early for whaling. One of the boats had reported seeing whales, but the beasts were shy, no doubt frightened off by the whaling ships.

But then there came a change in the weather; one day it was exceptionally good. Akiviak had observed that the ships had lowered their whaleboats; apparently they were already hunting.

"Let us go," said Kopak to Akiviak.

"We go!" repeated Akiviak in a whisper to the other members of the crew.

They shoved off to sea. It took time, for they had a long way to go. At long last Kopak spoke.

"Two of them are blowing straight ahead!" And then, a little later:

"I think we shall try!"

The oarsmen suddenly became much more careful with their oars. No one said a word. Akiviak was told to get ready. Then one of the whales came up to starboard, quite a distance away. Akiviak had loaded the new darting gun, which he was about to try for the first time. It was a simple large-caliber, short-barreled mortar attached to an ordinary harpoon handle, with a head made of iron. This harpoon head was attached to a long rope in the usual fashion. When the harpoon hit the whale the ignition mechanism was automatically released, causing the bomb projectile itself to be shot into the whale, where it exploded. At the same time the harpoon head became lodged in the whale, securing the catch.

Their course was just right. The whale came up ahead, close to the boat. Akiviak, who was standing with his darting gun raised ready to strike, threw it with such force that he almost fell into the sea. He saw the harpoon hit the whale in the neck; he heard the bang as the ignition went off and the shot was fired, and then he heard a thud from inside the animal. The whale convulsed violently, bouncing almost clear out of the water. Then it made a steep dive, pulling floats and towline with it. Akiviak held on to the bow of the boat, his eyes fixed on the floats. Suddenly, he felt the bow rising out of the sea and the boat keeled over to starboard. Akiviak turned and saw a baby whale coming up close under the boat. Quickly he grabbed the whale gun, the one which fired a bomb without a harpoon pointed the gun at the back of the whale, and fired from the hip. Blood poured from the back of the whale as it dived and disappeared. They let it go; they had to concentrate on catching the mother whale first.

They did get the mother, but the baby whale was gone. But that evening, as they were busy butchering the whale on the beach surrounded by the entire village, someone saw a whaleboat towing a baby whale in from the sea. In the back of the boat they could hear old man Olugat shouting the whale cry:

"Vo-ho-ho-hov!"

And Olugat, of all people! He, who had never caught a whale in his life! Were they seeing things? Kopak was the first man to voice what they were all thinking:

"That whale was probably dead when he found it, or else a miracle has happened!"

Kopak said this loud enough to be heard by all, for he suspected that it was probably their wounded baby whale which Olugat had found.

This caused a great deal of commotion among the people on the beach. They left the whale carcass where it was, and carrying their broad, greasy, slate flensing knives in their bloody hands, they flocked around Olugat's whaleboat as he came to beach his whale. In this way they spoiled the beaching ceremony to which he had so urgently looked forward. And his wife, poor thing, was left standing with her wooden bowl full of sour grass, without being allowed to play her part. Still, this was nothing compared to the blow dealt to Olugat's honor, now that he had at long last managed to get his whale. It naturally irked him that his fellow Eskimos failed to show him the honor he had so richly deserved; what was worse, he sensed their scepticism. That really hurt. As if he were incapable of catching a whale! He felt so humiliated that he couldn't even get cross. He had to pull himself together before he could show any signs of anger.

"Get out of the way! Move away and make room for our kill!"

Kopak let him beach his boat. Then he said:

"Tell me, Olugat. Where did you find this baby whale?"

This was an insult. To find a whale was not to kill a whale. But Olugat had to tell the truth, for his entire crew knew it. And it slipped out of him:

"It was floating on a floe!"

First there was silence. Then people started to laugh. It had to be a joke! Surely it was too funny to be true!

Kopak did not know what to think. At any rate the whale resembled the one they had shot, this he was sure of. But he could not resist the temptation to make fun of Olugat. He said:

"What are you saying? You don't mean to tell us that you scared the whale so that it jumped out of the sea and landed on a floe?"

It was now apparent that Olugat was beginning to feel insulted. But he was too talkative to be quiet.

"You may believe what you like. But it is as true as I am standing here. We found the whale lying on top of a floe of pack ice, and a floe that had been turned upside down at that.

Then Akiviak realized clearly what had happened. The wounded baby whale had dived under the pack ice, died, and floated up under an ice floe. When the pressure of the screw ice pushed together by wind and current, had capsized the floe, it had scooped the baby whale along with it. Thus, the whale was left on top of the floe. Quietly Akiviak went forward, and as the whale was pulled to the beach, he could see the wound in the beast's back where he had shot it. Before he could think, he said to Olugat so that every one could hear him:

"This whale *we* shot."

This was more than Olugat could take. He considered it a personal insult that he was accused of picking up a whale killed by others, and by a small kid at that. Olugat was known to be a man of ill temper; now he was furious. And now no one laughed any longer. One of the elders intervened by telling Olugat to hold his tongue. It was unworthy of men to meet quarreling. They had better settle their dispute in a manner more fitting to men of their station—with a song contest, as was the custom of their people and the tradition of their tribe. The insulted party, in that case Olugat, had to challenge the other party, Akiviak, to the duel of the drums.

Thus Akiviak was summoned to measure up against Olugat in a song contest, used by the ancient Eskimos to settle any disagreement between two men. It was a duel with words, the aim of which was to ridicule one another on the occasion of a traditional drum dance. The one who made the greatest fool of the other was the victor, judged by the amount of laughter from the audience.

This was a turn of events which Akiviak had not expected. After all, he had merely meant to bring to Olugat's attention that the whale which he had found, was one which he, Akiviak, had shot. This, according to ancient custom, entitled Akiviak's crew to half of the whale.

Many people were assembled in the karigi, for it had never happened before that a young boy had met an older man in a verbal competition. It started, according to ancient custom with an eating orgy. Olugat served as the host, and steaming hot boiled meat was passed around. He was obviously ill at ease as he sat there on the floor, exerting himself to live up to his (imagined) reputation of perfect host and gentleman. Akiviak, on the other hand, had nothing to lose. He chose to antagonize his opponent into losing his temper. He smiled innocently, then tried to look cute, sitting in front of his crew. Kopak sat in the back, with his goodhumored laughter, and a face full of smiles. Olugat's crew was seated on the opposite side, looking as if they actually enjoyed having fun at their captain's expense.

As soon as everyone had finished eating, the drummers seated themselves in the middle of the floor and started to hammer on the drums. They warmed up with some introductory songs. Then Olugat stepped forward, twiddled his drum and fumbled for words. Now he was obviously angry; he chose his statements uncritically. Without weighing his words he charged ahead, reminding his audience that the worst thing that could happen to a hunter was to lose his honor, his respect. This was the refrain throughout his whole singing presentation:

> *Hunters have here*
> *held their honor high,*
> *and all that was dear,*
> *or else they would die.*
> *This is the way it has been*
> *and has to be always!*

Then he went on to preach that what is right is right. Ever since the time of their great forefathers it had been the established rule that when a hunter found the carcass of a whale, he had to share it with his crew, and in addition give a generous share to those in the village who were old and to those unfortunate ones without providers. But could it be proved that the animal was actually killed by another man, that man was entitled to receive his equal share of the catch, and the hunter would give it to him gladly.

Then he banged on his drum and sang his refrain. The audience nodded and said that this was ture. Then Olugat went on and said something like this:

"It happened to us now that we found a whale the other day, floating on a floe. Imagine what a miracle it was to me and my men. A priceless catch, a whale, placed in our hands by the invisible spirits of the generous gods! We salvaged the whale and brought it to the beach, as you all now have seen, as a mountain of meat. And then comes this pup of a boy, arrogant, conceited and not yet a man. He makes us the laughingstock of the village by claiming that it was he who killed our whale. I can take a lot, but there is a limit, I tell you. Instead of acting like fools it is our duty to cut this pup down to size and put him in his place. He has to learn to hold his tongue, to guide his words more gently, and to honor, not ridicule, a man's reputation.

> *Hunters have here*
> *held their honor high*
> *and all that was dear*
> *or else they would die!*
> *This is the way it has been*
> *and has to be—always!"*

Thus Olugat ended the presentation of his case. He received only moderate applause as he marked the end of his song with a bang on his drum, and returned to his seat.

Now it was Akiviak's turn. He got up, hesitated slightly, played dumb, fumbled with the drum, and waited until it was absolutely still in the dance house. Then he took the floor and

sang, to voice his view and to present his case. In rough translation from his own tongue his epic verse went something like
this:

*"Here we have heard
the song of a saint,
the voice of a warrior,
violent words of wisdom!*

*Hailed as a hunter
Celebrated as a singer
Daring with his drum
is our old man Olugat!*

*Here I stand humbly,
in the shadow of his star
menaced by his might
I am merely a midget
with a trembling hand.*

*It is true what Olugat has told us.
Our people have had an ancient pact:
to share and share alike
a catch that is caught
by more than one man.*

*Long since, we have learned
that hardly a hunter
is braver or better
than my opponent, Olugat!*

*And since this is so,
tell me the truth:
What is the point or the purpose
in the mind of this man
to harbor such hatred
for a midget like me
who can hardly harm
such a hero as he?*

He would surely do better by sharing
instead of by having it all to himself:
For great is the man who has something to give,
and need not depend on the grace of his neighbor
to live on the catch some kid might have caught.

Such was the case here last summer,
the day I got home from a hunt
and kept the seal I had caught
strapped by a rope to a stone in the sea.
And when no one was watching
Olugat grabbed it.
He could at least have returned the rope!"

At this point Akiviak was interrupted by a outburst of hearty laughter from the audience. For everyone knew, though no one would openly say it, that Olugat had helped himself to a seal which Akiviak had killed and left tied to a stone by the shore. And as if this was not enough to make his opponent the laughingstock of the village Akiviak gaily went on with his song:

"And now we may turn
our attention to our task
and try to retrace
the ways of a whale.

It started like this, as I see it:
We had managed to hook
the harpoon in the mother.
Behind came her baby
tilting the boat with its tail.
But by then we had used
our gear on the mother,
had merely the whale gun
to use on the young one.
We fired, for we feared
it might break our boat.

We sensed a thud as the shell
went off with a bang in the whale.
When we went for the mother in the mist,
the young one sought safety under the ice,
finally it ended up under a floe.
When the floe toppled over with the tide
the baby was taken in the turn
and landed lying on the floe.
How else could a whale get on top of the ice?

In case there still may be men
who doubt and do not believe me,
see then for yourselves this fragment of the shell
which Kopak uncovered in Olugat's whale.
On it you see my grandfathers whale mark:
a cross in a ring resembling a scar.
This mark I made in the metal myself,
the hallmark we use on all Kopak's harpoons.

When the truth is to be told,
and this is my duty to do,
it cannot be questioned
that my statement is true.

Akiviak sat down. A roar of applause made it clear that the matter was settled. Akiviak was the victor, and a hero at that.

Kopak bought a phonograph with the money he obtained for the little whale bones.

VI

THE TRANSITION

THE following year no one caught any whales. In the fall two messengers came with an invitation to a messenger feast arranged by the inland people, the Nunamiuts, at the headwaters of the Oliktok River. The messengers arrived secretly and hid themselves in the hallway of Apayaok's house. When Apayaok came out and found the two masked men with their traditional painted sticks, he immediately sounded the alarm. People came running from all directions; then followed a mock fight between the messengers and the men of the village, in accordance with the traditional custom. Obviously, it was only in fun, for many of the village people were on the strangers' side, and "defended" them. Then all assembled in Apayaok's house to hear their message. And the envoys of the hosts in the mountains then recited the messages which they had learned by heart, giving details about who was invited, and what the hosts expected as gifts from each guest, and what the guests themselves might expect in return. In accordance with the number of rings painted on the messenger's sticks, ten main guests were to be invited. Apayaok and Kopak were among them. Kopak chose Akiviak as his runner. Akiviak's brother, Tigelok was chosen as runner for Apayaok. These two guests decided to travel together to the feast in the mountains in one boat; other guests did likewise. Even so, it amounted to quite a fleet of skin boats, filled with people and gifts, that rounded the sandspit at Point Barrow and continued east along the coast, to the point where the Colville River runs into the Arctic Ocean. There they took off and rowed up river, struggling against the swift current, pulling their boats over land to get by some of the most difficult rapids. They camped on the beach every night and slept under the up-turned boats which served as their shelter. In the evenings when the weather was good they sat around their campfire singing, practicing the particular dance steps which they were to perform during the festival.

The river became narrower as the days passed, and swifter. Eventually they came to the place where the Oliktok and Colville rivers meet, and they continued up the Oliktok. Akiviak began to recognize the country, the flat fields of tundra around Umiat, the foothills of the Utukok Mountains, where he had lived as a child. The sight of autumn-colored heather, the gentle breeze down the mountain slopes, the familiar sight of a fleeing caribou . . . he was overcome by a feeling of belonging to this country, the place of his origin.

Towards the end of the journey the river ran too swiftly, and the going became too rough for the boat. They pulled it out of the water and left it on land and continued on foot along the west bank of the river, carrying the heavy bundles bearing their precious gifts on their backs. They walked together, single file. After having camped four nights in the mountains, they came to the stone cairn on the hill above Umiat, a mile or so south of the Oliktok, where the Nunamiuts lived. Here again they camped. In the night the two messenger-men who had accom-

panied them from Point Barrow took off to report to the hosts
that their guests were approaching. The following day Akiviak
observed a group of boys, ten in all, who came running out from
the settlement and up the hillside. Each carried a short stick,
and as they reached the cairn, out of breath, they lined up in
a row. One by one they called the name of the particular guest
who was to race back to camp with them. But the guests chose
to be represented by their own runners, who stepped forward
and paired up the host runners. Then they all sat down in the
heather. Each of them was given a piece of dried meat to eat.
When this was done the runners got up and walked in a circle
around the guests, singing a ceremonial song. Suddenly one of
them started to run. This was the signal for all the runners to
take off. Thus they raced all the way to the Nunamiut camp, the
principal guests themselves jogging along. As it turned out the
guest runners arrived first; consequently the guests were masters
of the dance tent and won the privilege of being the first to
dance.

When they had celebrated four days on end, everyone gathered on the tundra a distance away from the camp. They lined
up and counted—atasi, aipuk, pingayuak—and then all of them
raced back to the dance tent. Tigelok came first, and got a chunk
of tallow as a prize. Finally the guests received their parting gifts
and started on their return journey.

On the way home, disaster struck. Many of them fell ill with
high fever, loss of appetite, weakness, and a terrible hacking
cough. They developed a rash all over their bodies. Some of
them barely dragged themselves along to the boats. Those who
were well had to carry the packs for those who were sick. Akiviak
too was affected, but was able to take care of himself. Kopak, on
the other hand, could hardly keep up with the rest. On the way
downriver he got worse. He had difficulty breathing, his lips
looked blue. He suffered from high fever and hallucinations.
Before the day was over he was dead. At the foot of a rocky slope

they left his body, wrapped in the caribou skin which Kopak had received as a gift from his host at Oliktok.

But it did not end here. As they camped the following evening by the fire, sad and discouraged, they saw a skin boat drifting down the river with nothing but dead bodies on board. During the night Apayaok too became ill. Feverish, he babbled incoherently and ranted like a madman. In the morning he was unable to get up. When they started to carry their gear on board he asked to be left behind. They tried to change his mind, but in vain. Finally he had to be carried on board. In the bottom of the umiak the old hunter fell on his knees, praying to his new Christian God in a feeble, barely audible voice. Sweat dripped from his forehead onto his folded hands. He prayed for peace for his soul. Akiviak watched the old man in silence, this old respected leader who was looked up to and admired by all, who was now begging for help from someone he had never seen, but believed in.

By nightfall Apayaok said he felt better.

By now there were four boats, with only half their crews left. The rest were dead. Eventually the storm which had left them stranded and short of food, subsided sufficiently to allow them to continue. But the sea was still very rough. Wind flurries swept like shadows along the waves. The umiak rocked like a washbasin on the angry sea. They paddled with all the strength they could muster. Finally Akiviak became sick, and lay down in the bottom of the boat vomiting without even trying to lean over the side as he threw up. He felt so utterly indifferent to life or death that if anyone had attempted to throw him overboard he would not have resisted. The boat was heaving. He felt as if his intestines were sliding back and forth every time the boat rolled. As he lay suffering he saw the old man Apayaok kneel down in the bow, raising his strong hands against the sky, praying to the Lord for help; he saw his white head against the sky; it rose and fell with the sea. Akiviak remembered a picture of a monk he had seen in the church, and recalled the schoolteacher's story of the disciples who were afraid, and about the Lord who stilled the storm on the Sea of Galilee. Then he passed out. When he regained consciousness the umiak, was afloat in calm waters. Apayaok and Tigelok pulled in at a cove, where they spent the night. The following day it started to blow again; it was out of the question to put out to sea. Tigelok went out with his rifle and shot a seagull, which they cooked and ate. The following day he shot an owl, which they ate raw. The third day he caught a fox. This was all they had to eat. They decided to leave the boat where it was and continue on foot along the coast. After having walked for two days they came to a tent, near a river. There they stayed a few days to rest, eat and to regain their strength. Then they were taken across the river, and continued on their journey west to Point Barrow. In the evening they arrived at still another river which blocked their way. They followed the east bank inland until they came upon a fishing camp. Here again they stayed a few days, living on fish which they caught in the river. Then they went on.

They walked and they walked, how long, no one knew, for they no longer counted the days. At last they came far enough to recognize the landscape, staggering on by sheer willpower in the loose sand. Whenever possible they walked along the water's edge where there was a better foothold. Thus they pulled ahead, trudging around the lagoon towards Point Barrow. At sundown they saw the village as a speck far in the distance, the houses silhouetted against the evening sky. The sun gleamed like a copper disc on the horizon. Not a sound, not even a barking dog could be heard.

A slight breeze blew in from the west, bringing with it the smell of burned blubber and peat from the fireplaces. This was a sign of life; but there was no smoke to be seen, nor any people, nor activity of any kind. Nothing but emaciated dogs that wandered loose between the houses. In the grass by an underground meat cellar lay dead bodies, fully dressed, as if they had collapsed as they walked. A little distance away was a heap of turf from an open grave. The worst fears of the returning men were now confirmed. Their anxiety soon became terror. Outside one of the houses they met an old woman they knew. She told them about the terrible sickness that had struck the village. Very many people had died, more than half the population was gone. Many of the Eskimos were still sick. Kopak's wife was alive, but the old woman with whom they spoke had no knowledge about the rest of their relatives. By the church they met Akiviak's sister, Sila, looking thin and pale; she was crying.

Thus ended the messenger festival, the last one in that part of the country. The catastrophe was caused by a sickness which came with the foreigners from the south and spread along the coast, along the main route of communication, mercilessly wiping out entire households, and destroying many villages.

Akiviak went home to Kopak's wife with the tragic news. Not much was said between the two, but Akiviak sensed what she was thinking: it was all the foreigners' fault, who had angered the old gods and brought their vengeance down on the people.

Some time later a supply ship anchored up outside the lagoon. In the night a violent storm broke out from the north, ramming the ice against the shore. The supply ship drifted aground and was wrecked, the crew was rescued. It was late in the fall and no other vessels would come to Point Barrow that year. The crew therefore had to spend the winter in the village. They split up and went to stay with different families: the captain came to live with the trader, the mate with the missionary, and the boatsman with Takpuk, the brother of Apayaok. The rest of the crew had to stay in the church. Unavoidably these strangers left their imprints upon this primitive society; the foreign influence was now permanently upon them, for better or for worse. Akiviak saw how difficult it was for a tribe like his to maintain its identity, to preserve its culture and integrity. In reality most of the Eskimos, the young ones in particular, admired the foreigners and tried very hard to emulate them. At the same time the foreigners created unrest and bad feelings wherever they came, as was the case when the captain helped himself to an Eskimo woman without her husband's consent. This was unheard of, an insult to the Eskimo husband, a violation of his honor, and a serious breach of an ancient custom which said that no one makes passes at a wife behind her husband's back. Nor does one borrow another man's wife without the husband's explicit consent. Thus the captain had committed a crime in the eyes of the whole village; the people cried for vengeance, some even demanding the captain's life in payment. But it was the poor Eskimo woman who was punished after all; she was spanked by her husband outside their house, humiliated in the presence of many people.

The boatsman did not behave any better, he who was accommodated by Takpuk. Takpuk had two wives, and he politely offered his own wife number two to the boatsman. But the boatsman was greedy, and one day when Takpuk was out hunting, he took advantage of wife number one as well. Akiviak happened to drop in, and found the boatsman on top of the woman on the sleeping platform. Akiviak backed out of the doorway and collided with wife number two, who came from the shore, hauling a seal carcass with a rope. Akiviak pointed at the actors on the bed and said, "They are busy!" The woman took one look through the door, then ran over to the neighbor's, and when Takpuk returned from his hunt, it was known all over Barrow that the boatsman had played him for a fool. The boatsman had to get out of the house and join the crew at the church.

That winter there was famine in Point Barrow. The whaling had failed completely, as did the seal hunt to some extent. There were few foxes with which to purchase imported food in the store. The trader had long ago refused any more credit. Without fox skins or any other products in demand, no one could obtain either flour or tea from the store.

Akiviak still stayed with the widow of his stepfather Kopak and provided for her. He had his fox traps set on the tundra, but as a rule they were empty whenever he went to check them. And even though there might be the occasional seal out on the ice, it was usually impossible to get after them because of bad weather.

Akiviak's sister, Sila, had married the fellow who worked as the full-time storekeeper for the trader; he was a foreigner and his skin was white as snow. They lived in a log house next to the store. Akiviak visited them daily, emptied their toilet bucket, and served whatever useful purpose he could. For this he was given leftovers from their table. His sister secretly gave him extra food to take home as well. When he was particularly thrifty, he was allowed to work for the missionary's wife too. He brought ice from the lake for drinking water, did odd jobs, and cleaned up in the church. There he met Sussi. Her name was actually Sila; she was the daughter of Olugat's brother. She worked as a maid for the missionary's wife, a job Akiviak's sister had had before she got married.

True enough, he had met Sussi before. But somehow he had not noticed her. Then it happened one day when he was bringing in a sledload of fresh-water ice. He knocked on the kitchen door and waited. Then out came a young woman. She swung the door wide open and bent forward to look down at him as he stood by the doorstep. The first thing Akiviak noticed was her eyes; they shone with an inviting sensuality and intelligence. He thought that he detected the flash of a smile about her mouth, a twitching in her full, sensitive lips. Best of all, she had dimples. She stood in the doorway above him, her body so fine and slender that he developed strange sensations in his own. Then he saw the cross hanging on a string around her neck.

"Come in," she said, then turned around and went in, closing the door behind her. He waited a while outside on the doorstep before he entered, as was customary, probably in order to give those inside time to prepare themselves for their guest. When Akiviak entered with a large chunk of ice cradled in his arms, she was standing by the kitchen bench, cleaning a tray.

"You work here?" he said. He felt he had to say something.

"And you carry ice?"

Yes, that he did. What else could he say?

He placed the ice in the fresh-water drum, made several trips, and filled the drum. Then he looked around to see if there was anything else he could do, as an excuse to stay on, but found nothing and prepared to go.

"Well, is there anything else?" he asked.

"No, there is nothing more."

"I see."

He walked backward out through the door. But the encounter had whetted his appetite.

Now he started to attend the church service in the evenings. He was inquisitive, and he had nothing better to do. And besides, Sussi was there. She was always to be found in the front row.

But it was Apayaok's confession that turned out to be of decisive importance to Akiviak's spiritual future. For here the young Akiviak saw the famed hunter Apayaok, white-haired and dignified, turn to the congregation and tell them, in their own language, about his meeting with the new God. How he, as a heathen, had followed gods that did not exist, how he in vain had sought refuge and help from the spirits of his ancestors, worshipped dead objects, believed in nonsense and witchcraft. How he, from being a doubting man, a man without faith, came to believe in the Lord and found the creator of earth and heaven, who sacrificed His own son to save their souls. In a divine revelation he received the Christian message, was given the gift to communicate with the Holy Spirit, was blessed with the spirit of brotherly love, and found peace within himself in conviction of the existence of life after death. He was now a servant to the will of the Almighty.

While Apayaok spoke it was absolutely still in the room. People were taken by his message, for it had something to offer everyone, it seemed. There was much to gain and very little to lose in this new faith; as it promised a better life after the one they were now living, it was no doubt worth taking a chance. Especially as long as they, at the same time, could carry their amulets, consult the stone that caused the wind to blow in the right direction, and keep the old gods in reserve. Then they might well take the risk of being without a shaman, at least for the time being. But for Akiviak this new religion became something much more than mere faith. It provided an explanation for creation itself, the realization of an element of God in all living matter, an insight into the true character of nature. There was now a deeper meaning to life, a basis for hope in the long run. He reasoned with himself:

"Perhaps there is a meaning in everything. And if events may seem meaningless, it is probably because of my own lack of insight." He kept pondering about these problems while the missionary's wife played the zither and Sussi sang "All things bright and beautiful."

He attended Sunday school. Biblical history interested him deeply. Naive as he was, he found the stories of the Bible simple and natural. The accounts fascinated him; he developed them further with the aid of his own imagination. Receptive as his mind was, he was easily affected by the Christian ethics: "Do unto your neighbor as you will that he shall do unto you," the missionary's wife had said. But this was precisely what his mother had told him to do, yet she was a heathen. As biblical history was revealed to him and he developed it further in his own mind, he felt he could recognize in it his own society. The trader became the Pharisee, and his own tribe became God's chosen people. He allowed himself to be carried away by his own argumentation and sentiment. Now he saw clearly that he had a mission: he was to go out and make Christians of all, so that they might meet the arriving foreigners in the spirit of Christ.

With the Christian faith came also the Christian commandments: "You shall rest on the seventh day," the Sunday school teacher had told them. But for the Eskimos it was hard to let a seal go by, even on a Sunday. Then they were told that it was a sin to have more than one wife, even though the second wife was only a maid in the house and the husband could support them both. What, then, should they do, those who already had more than one wife? For it was also a sin to send the second one away. Take, for instance the amiable hunter Suki, who was converted to Christianity. His dearest wife was old, had trouble with her legs and had difficulty moving about. It was no longer possible for her to accompany Suki when he went to the camp to fish in the summer, and had to live in a tent; so he had always brought along wife number two to do the housekeeping for him. What should he do now? First he asked the missionary for advice, but got no sense from him. Then he talked it over with his wives. They saw no other way out than for him to divorce his old wife for the duration of the summer fishing season, and to officially marry wife number two for that period. Then he had to divorce wife number two when he returned home, remarry wife number one, and let divorced wife number two stay in the house as their guest.

And then there were the blessed occasions when the Eskimos, in keeping with their old traditions, blew out the oil lamps and swapped wives in the dark, for better or for worse. As a consequence there were hardly any families without children. But this also had to be brought to an end, for all this was sin, said the missionary. Even the drum dance was frowned upon, but this no one could touch, for it was a joyful and inseparable part of their life.

Even the dogs suffered under the new order. They had always in the past been allowed to go loose. They consumed everything that came their way, even that which the humans left in the form of droppings. Thus the dogs served as some kind of garbage collectors, and it was fairly clean around the houses. Understandably, this stool consumption upset the missionary; he made the Eskimos keep their dogs tied up. The result was a dirty village with a most objectionable odor. But even this the Eskimos got used to, a testament to the remarkable adaptability of the human race.

The worst part, however, was a new thing called hell. This threat of eternal punishment was something completely novel. True enough, they were used to being bothered by evil spirits. They were frightened by the power of the angakok (witch doctor), but his curse did not last forever. And while in the past their ancestors had died peacefully, knowing that the soul was released from the body at death, they now got the fear of hell instead. However, Akiviak had taken particular note of what the missionary called "the Grace of God." He was counting heavily on the forgiveness of his sins, and for this reason too he did believe in eternal life.

"I hear you are saved," said Apayaok to Akiviak one day. Akiviak fancied hearing this from Apayaok, for it made him feel that he was in good company.

Akiviak was already known for his talents and respected for his skills. The fact that he had in addition become a genuine Christian automatically opened new possibilities for him. The missionary made use of his services more often, and he was the paid handyman in the school. Then he became an assistant to the teacher, but had to quit school during the whaling season, for now he was also captain on one of the trader's whaleboats, even though he was only 17 summers old. He now decided it was about time to start his own family, for now he could really use a wife. Sexual sensations and bodily urges he had had for a good many years, but these could easily be relieved by rubbing against the girls standing by the walls outside the houses in the dark. But as a wife of lasting value Sussi had appeared as a natural choice, and now was the time. With his older brother Tigelok he went to Sussi's father, Takpuk, and presented his case, but the old man said only this:

"The day you are worthy you will have my daughter—perhaps!"

That was all he got, not even an offer to move over to Takpuk's house and work for his daughter, as was the old custom. However, in all fairness, there might be good reasons for this: in the first place Akiviak already had his own boat crew, and Takpuk had his. Secondly they had become Christians by now and all marrying had to take place with the singing of psalms and a wedding in the church.

As it turned out, two years passed before Akiviak was allowed to wed his Sussi. It happened the year he was 19, and had returned from a successful whale hunt in the spring. Then the girl's mother took the initiative and let it be known that it certainly would not be against her wishes if Akiviak got Sussi. So the two of them went together to Takpuk, who cleared his throat and spat, and thought for a while before he answered that there was probably nothing he could do about it; they'd better have it their way!

And so, during the whaling festival in the fall, the two of them were tossed into the air on a walrus hide, landed on all fours, and were pronounced man and wife in the Christian manner by the missionary. They danced and beat their drums the whole wedding night, even though the missionary said it was a sin. This joy they had to allow themselves, for that much respect they owed to the old gods. They built a house from driftwood in the shadow of the church and settled on the earthen floor just before the snow came.

By now things had become very lively in Point Barrow. People from all places and of all kinds: traders, sailors, Lapps with domesticated reindeer. Several different missionaries came, each one representing a different interpretation of the Bible, competing with one another for the few Eskimo souls they all wanted to save. Some of the sects observed Sunday, others had chosen Saturday as their holy day of worship and rest. The Eskimos hardly knew what to believe. Now the boats with crews from both congregations could hunt only five days a week. This had a bad effect on their livelihood.

In the middle of this period of transition a foreigner arrived in Point Barrow with some very ambitious plans. He was to establish a whole chain of stores along the coast from Point Barrow to Canada. He hired Akiviak as his interpreter. Thus Akiviak gained an insight into the methods used by the foreigners, and a better idea of their views on the Eskimos. He saw that they took advantage of every opportunity to profit at the Eskimos expense. Old Nakajok, for example, was an excellent trapper who always had a lot of fox skins hanging in his hallway. One day he boarded the trader's boat with a sackful of skins. He brought out one skin at a time, and sold them one by one to the highest bidder, collecting his payment at once, until the sack was empty. But then the captain played a dirty trick on him. He started the engine, pulled up the anchor and left. The Eskimo had to rush to his boat, leaving most of his goods behind.

Then it happened one night in Point Barrow that Akiviak was awakened by a terrible shout. He went out and saw that the church was on fire. The flames roared against the sky, bright as daylight.

Hell, thought Akiviak. It had to be hell, for this was precisely the way the missionary had described it. Akiviak froze, his heart pounding. The devil was loose, he was sure; this was the final night of justice. And in the church of all places! He had better stay out of it, he thought to himself. Frightened, he sneaked back into his bunk and hid himself under the bed skins behind Sussi. But when he saw that people ran to the burning church with buckets of water, he realized he was safe. He joined them and took part in the hopeless task of putting out the fire. But the church burned to the ground. In the ashes they found the body of the old shaman Kuklok, who was hard of hearing. Akiviak could not help thinking: could it be that the Lord wanted to punish those who failed Him, and who faltered in their faith, and kept to the shaman Kuklok and the old omens? Or was it the old gods that had come to take revenge, the spirits from the not too distant past who had led them for so long, and now wanted to shake them up for loss of faith and failure to follow the ways of their forefathers? For a while Akiviak was unable to decide which was the case. Then the missionary returned. He said Satan was behind the fire. That settled it, for it had to be the truth if the missionary said so.

In the new radio station at Barrow, the radio operator was ticking away a message about the fire. That summer new building materials arrived from Seattle, and they started to rebuild the church. And this is how Akiviak happened to become a carpenter. He had never used a saw before, nor seen a hammer, to say nothing about hitting a nail. But he was handy, and had a gift for practical work. However, he never bothered to measure anything accurately; he simply cut the boards using his eyesight and his judgment. To measure a board which was to fit in an open space under a window, he used his hands and kept them that far apart, walked over to the board and cut it that long.

Consequently, the result was somewhat haphazard and by no means as tight as the missionary had wanted. But perhaps there was some truth in what Akiviak said: "It had better not be completely airtight in the house of the Lord, for how else could the Holy Spirit get in when the door is closed, if not through the cracks in the wall?"

However, it turned out that there was not enough material to finish the church, and it was never really completed. They patched it up the best they could with bits and pieces, they could find, added odd skins here and there to make it fairly draft-free, and used it as it was. But they said the church was haunted. When the weather was bad and it was windy, they could hear someone knocking in the night. Someone had seen flashing lights inside the church. Probably it was the devil himself, and the restless soul of the shaman, thought Akiviak, and strung a cross around his neck for safety's sake.

The following year a cutter came to Point Barrow on its way east to Canada with supplies. They needed a man, and Akiviak signed up as a stoker. He left his wife at Point Barrow; she was pregnant. But he was not at all happy as a sailor. In the first place he was always seasick, and even though he prayed until he stopped throwing up, he still felt nauseated every time the weather was bad and the ship rolled. Besides, he never got used to going to sleep in shifts. Four hours' sleep was not enough for a man used to sleeping until it pleased him to wake up. All in all, to be a stoker was not a suitable occupation for a hunter. Every time he opened the door to the boiler and saw the roaring flames he immediately thought of the church fire, and of hell. When the ship finally anchored up outside the lagoon on its return to Point Barrow, Akiviak was the first to get ashore. He almost left without his pay.

As he came running up from the beach, Akiviak saw a funeral procession on its way to the burial ground. The two men in front carried a long pole over their shoulders from which a small bundle was suspended. Behind them came people whom Akiviak recognized as his relatives. He was puzzled. Who could it be that they carried to the grave now? He ran on. At home he found Sussi, lying on her bunk, pale, almost a shadow of herself. He got scared when he saw how thin she was; she had been pregnant, and in good shape, when he left. Sussi leaned on her elbows and said:

"She was born last night. She died this morning. They have just carried her to the grave."

It was her, then, that they carried in the bundle—his daughter, who was to be named Dorka. Akiviak remained standing inside the door. He hesitated: should he run after them to the grave, or should he stay there with Sussi? He was filled with guilt. Then a passage from the scriptures came to him: Let the dead bury the dead.

And Sussi sighed softly: "It is all in the hands of the Lord."

Akiviak turned to the open door. The evening sun threw long shadows towards the burial hill. There, near where his mother lay, they had placed his newborn child. He thought: "From the tundra did you come; to the sod shall you return."

On the flat fields he saw bright yellow poppies swaying in the wind. He turned around and sat down beside Sussi. Neither of them cried.

This marked the end of Akiviak's stay at Point Barrow. With the salary he had earned as a sailor he bought himself a wooden whaleboat, fully equipped, and prepared to move. He had seen much game on his trip to Canada. Now he would travel to the east, his next of kin with him, start afresh and found a settlement of his own, preaching the gospel on the way. This was the same dream of so many before him, all those who broke from the old established society to build something better. And history repeats itself each time: for man remains the same. He carries the old human nature with him wherever he goes. And whatever he creates in the way of a society around himself, he creates as an image of himself. He would not be human otherwise.

But Akiviak had made up his mind. The missionary, hearing of his plans, went to him:

"I hear you want to leave us, son."

Akiviak faced him:

"I have a mission to perform." This pleased the missionary, for he heard his own voice speaking. He said with enthusiasm, "I have seen that you are gifted. But take your time, prepare yourself first for your task. You come to me and I will show you the way."

And so it happened that Akiviak completed a missionary course at Point Barrow, taught by the missionary himself. It turned out to be a private tutoring course in the evenings, lasting all winter long. Thus they worked their way through the Apostles' Creed, confession of the Christian faith, and all of the shorter catechism. Akiviak struggled with the letters; the missionary explained and simplified. The pupil had to learn the scriptures by heart. Once a week he had to take a test. He pulled small pieces of paper out of a hat on which were written the numbers of chapter and verse. Akiviak was then expected to repeat the scripture, word for word, from memory. His teacher persisted, and did not give up until Akiviak was qualified. Then one day Akiviak received a letter from the head office of the mission back in the United States. He was now a preacher.

VII

THE DAWN
OF A NEW DAY

THEY started the journey to the east in the middle of the
summer, first Akiviak and Tigelok in the whaleboat, together
with their families. Then followed three skin boats with relatives
and a group of volunteers who felt the need for a change. The
boats were filled with all that they owned: dogs, sleds, utensils
and food. They left quietly, without fanfare or fuss of any
kind.

Already the first day they encountered trouble: a strong gale
from the north which pushed the pack ice towards land, blocking their way. Before nightfall they had to seek shelter behind
a reef. The water was too shallow for them to get ashore, so they
spent the night in their boats. They spent several days waiting
for the weather to improve. They ran out of drinking water, and
Akiviak suggested they might pray to the Lord for help. The
following morning a small floe of pack ice came floating by, so
close that it almost scraped the boat; from this they broke off
a chunk of fresh-water ice from the top. They praised the
Lord.

When at long last they were about to cross the Ikpikpuk fjord, the fog was so thick that they lost sight of the other boats. When it suddenly lifted they were staring straight into the bow of a cutter steaming from the opposite direction. It almost ran them down. And when the visibility improved enough to establish contact with the rest of the party, they discovered that one of the boats was missing, the one belonging to Paneak and his family. There was nothing they could do about it, so they continued.

There was more trouble when they tried to cross the broad stretch of open water outside the mouth of the Colville River. They ran into a storm, and had difficulty staying together. The breakers rolled over the shallow underwater reefs, waves so high that they hid the sun. During some of the wind squalls the breakers rolled over the gunwale and threatened to fill the boat. It almost capsized when a large breaker unexpectedly hit from the side. By now they had drifted far towards land, into danger-ously shallow waters. Tigelok tied himself to the bow and lay flat on his stomach, constantly measuring the depth of the water with a weight tied to the end of a rope. They followed a channel about four fathoms deep until they reached shelter behind an island, where they landed. They saw a flock of ducks on the beach. The youngsters wanted to shoot them for food, but Akiviak asked them not to even though they were hungry, for it was Sunday.

They continued struggling in stops and starts, at the mercy of the weather. On the coast near a place they named Kuparuk, they ran into hunters who had come from the east and had settled there by a ness. Here they had a chance to rest, dry their clothing, and repair the damage to the boats before pressing on to the east. Finally, one day they had come far enough to see the sand reefs west of Kaktoavik. But then the wind blew in from the southwest, and the current came in the opposite direction. It was impossible to sail or row around the reefs on the outside.

There was only one thing to do: try and get through the shallow channel inside the sand bars. But here it was so shallow in places that the wooden whaleboat hit the bottom every time it came down on a wave. The lighter skin boats, on the other hand, stayed afloat and got through. They therefore anchored the umiaks and pulled the whaleboat with a towline over the worst parts, while Akiviak and his crew used their long poles to help push the boat ahead. They sailed along the coast inside some small islands around a long sandspit, and into a lagoon in the evening. There they floated on two fathoms of water and were sheltered by the land. The wind died down. The sun was setting in the sea. They were surrounded by a ring of white sand beaches. Beyond the beach they could see niggerheads covered with poppies that swayed in the breeze. A fox was barking on top of a stone. A caribou was feeding further in. The cry of a loon rose from a lake, a flock of ducks passed overhead; there were seals in the water.

Sussi stood up in the boat, shadowed her eyes with her hand, looked around, and said:

"Here I want to stay!"

"Then we stay here!" said Akiviak.

The place was called Kaktoavik, a peninsula in the Arctic Ocean separated from the mainline by a ford, where one could walk across at low tide.

They went ashore and found an abundance of driftwood, especially on the north side of the sandspit. Akiviak realized that they had been lucky, for this was a most suitable place to build a settlement.

"This must be the place the Lord has picked," he thought to himself.

They put up frames of driftwood resting on slabs of stone, covered the walls and roof with peat, and packed sand around the base of the houses to make them warmer. But then Akiviak had the misfortune to cut himself with the axe; this excluded him from any further physical work. But he could still supervise. When all the igloos were about finished, Akiviak climbed the hill just behind the houses. There he remained standing until dusk, waiting for the moon to rise, watching the lights from the homes twinkle under a glowing sky. The sea burned with a golden flame where the sun had gone down. A slight movement of cool air stirred the wolverine trimmings on Akiviak's parka hood. He had the evening sky in his eyes. From the corners of his mouth a smile spread over his face. He was filled with joy. "This is the closest I have ever been to heaven," he thought to himself.

Here he saw the beginning of a new society. Here he was to experience the final transition to a new era.

While it was still summer and the ground was unfrozen, Akiviak started to dig; he was going to make a food cellar in a mound close to the house. The digging went easier than he had expected, so he figured that he might as well dig two cellars while he was at it. For now he was going to teach his clan how to use a larder the way the foreigners did. Sussi was puzzled:

"What do we need two meat cellars for? We hardly have any food to store in the first place."

But Akiviak was optimistic, as was his nature:

"As long as you have a cellar, you will always have food!"

But this was not necessarily the case, for Akiviak, like most of his people, had never really learned to save for a rainy day or to keep his larder filled. He ate more than enough in times of plenty, and starved as a matter of course when there was nothing to eat, referring to the scriptures: "The Lord who feeds the sparrow will provide us, too, with our daily bread."

In the fall they went upriver to fish for trout and hunt caribou on the tundra. They returned in October with a lot of meat, making several trips to bring it all home.

As soon as the sea froze along the shore they hunted seal.

Once they returned with over 50 seals and a polar bear after a day's hunt. Sussi was busy preparing the meat. She cut it in long strips which she put into pokes filled with seal oil. In the end she had ten such pokes lying on the roof. This was her way of making a larder, a way as old as the tribe itself.

During the late fall and most of the winter they trapped foxes, placing their traps on the brink along the coast and on hillocks along the river where the wind would keep the ground bare of snow. There were many foxes; some trappers caught as many as twenty in a single day. Akiviak himself had well over fifty fox skins hanging in the shed long before Christmas. And the price was quite good. Earlier a skin would fetch about $20, corresponding to the price of two sacks of flour. Now they got as much as $60 a piece when they sold their pelts on board the supply ship in the summer. Then they heard that the trader at Cape Herschel in Canada paid more. This was a good enough reason for going there, even though it took a month. They needed little excuse to make a journey, for they thrived on company. And so it happened that Akiviak, with his entire household, went to Cape Herschel with a load of pelts on his sled. He brought his bible along, and preached on his way. He became known as the apostle of the fox skins.

At the time of Akiviak's arrival at Cape Herschel the villagers were in the middle of building a hospital. This was something that interested Akiviak. It so happened that there was a job for him as a carpenter at a rate of $4 an hour. This was the going wage for a carpenter at Cape Herschel, quite a bit more than the salary of a preacher. The families decided to remain at Cape Herschel for the winter, hammering away at the hospital. Here Akiviak witnessed the white leaders of the project hammering away at each other as well. The building foreman fell out with the missionary over a question of priority: which was more important, the hospital or the church? It ended with the foreman receiving an ecclesiastical bang on the head from the missionary, (the foreman ended up in the hospital,) the missionary nursing a black eye, and no church.

They spent Christmas at Cape Herschel and saw Santa Claus climb down through the smoke hole in the meeting house roof to distribute candy to the kids. Then they all ate together from an assortment of food brought by members of the congregation. They played games and held dog races on the ice, and concluded with a drum dance.

The winter was almost gone by the time they returned to Kaktoavik, their sleds loaded with flour. And when the sun was high enough they went out on the ice to hunt seal, pushing the rifle in front of them on a sled rigged with a white sail, behind which they hid themselves while crawling along on their stomachs. In this way, hiding behind the sled, they surprised the seal as it sunned itself on the ice by the edge of the breathing hole. There were days when the hunters caught as many as ten seals each.

By now Kaktoavik had grown into quite a village, with a clan of permanent settlers, permanent because they had invested too much labor and capital in their homes to abandon them and to go elsewhere. They had also grown accustomed to a certain amount of comfort and equipment, some of which was too heavy or bulky to bring along on a sled, and which they would prefer not to be without. For this reason too they felt compelled to remain where they were. But even so they had to travel; they had to move a bit, to visit people and see friends, for such was their nature. Whenever a traveling party came by there was always someone ready to join them. They usually stayed with relatives or friends on the way; they might stay for months, living as non-paying guests. Time was of no consequence; they had plenty of it. Thus they never hurried. When the fishing or hunting was better somewhere else, they went there for a while, alone or in a group. They might go to the fishing camp in the summer, or to a temporary hunting shelter in the fall.

More people followed, and joined the families at Kaktoavik. Most of them came from the west, like Sussi's parents and Akiviak's younger brother, Kanayuk, and his sister Sila who was married to the white storekeeper. Others came from the east. Gradually the settlement expanded, at times becoming quite crowded. This hurt the seal hunting, for apparently all the fuss and noise frightened the animals away from the village. Alert and very sensitive, they were very hard to catch. Besides, there were more hunters now who took their share of the seal population; consequently the number of seals, dwindled, and with it the amount of catch.

The village centered around Akiviak, the obvious head of the clan, he who was both hunter and storyteller, shaman and preacher, magician and interpreter, drum dancer and singer and maker of songs.

One day in the spring, at the time of the thaw, a dogsled with a group of Eskimos arrived. It was Paneak and his family, who had been lost in the fog on the Ikpikpuk fjord on their first voyage to Kaktoavik. An ice floe had torn a hole in the bottom of their skin boat, which sank. They barely managed to climb onto the floe. A storm came, waves so huge that they blocked the moon. The floe broke in two; then the edges kept breaking off by the action of the waves. In the end it was so small that it barely supported their weight. They drifted about for weeks, living on seals which they shot and retrieved with a weighted throwing hook attached to the end of a long rope. At times they came so close to land that they could see caribou grazing on the landbrink. When the fall came and they had given up every hope of being saved, the weather suddenly turned very cold and calm. Overnight the sea around them froze, and they walked ashore on the new ice; they made their way back to Point Barrow on foot along the coast. But by then the Spanish flu had reached Barrow; it had come from the south. Most of the Eskimos at

Point Barrow got sick; some of them survived and slowly regained their health. Others never recovered. There was hardly a house without a dead body. The living buried the dead in open graves in the permafrost, which they thawed with the help of steam and fire. Paneak lost a son, Timarok, the boy who was born on the tundra.

The summer passed uneventfully, but in the course of the winter they ran out of food. They had neither flour, sugar, or tea. So they harnessed their dogs and went all the way to Cape Herschel to purchase the necessary supplies. In the spring the hunting was good, and all was well. When the supply ship arrived in the summer, Akiviak bought a large supply of flour in addition to sugar, coffee, tea, fruit and a lot of canned goods. As time passed they ate more of the imported food than their own and left the empty cans in heaps around their houses. Eventually it became a habit, and they had to have this kind of food.

While before they had lived off the land and managed quite well on their simple regimen, they were now the slaves of a complicated money system based on exchange of goods. Previously they themselves had made their implements and tools from material which they found on land, and from the animals which they caught; now they had to hand over their catch for the food they needed. The more they needed, the more they had to hunt. And the more they hunted, the more ammunition they had to have. And this they had to buy, so they had to hunt more also on this account. This was all very well as long as there was enough game. But when the game disappeared and the hunting failed, they were in trouble. And the greater they grew in numbers, the more of them suffered when the basis for their existence failed.

As with Akiviak. He started to hunt foxes with traps of wood which he made himself. In exchange for the foxes he bought flour, tea, sugar, coffee and canned food. But in addition, he had to buy ammunition which he needed to hunt caribou and seal. But the more purchased food he consumed, the less he had left for ammunition. And the less ammunition, the less meat he ate. It was a vicious circle. In the end they lived on nothing but flour, as long as there were foxes to trap. Soon the foxes had been exploited completely; and when the foxes were gone they could no longer get flour either. Then they had to think of something new: they started to hunt wolves for a cash bounty. But since the hunting of wolves took most of their time, they hardly had time left over for hunting seal and caribou. Consequently they lived mostly on purchased food. Finally they ended up using most of their spare time traveling to and from the store to buy food.

The result was that instead of greater security with the new weapons and the improved living standard, they became more and more insecure. Those whom it hit hardest were the women, like Sussi:

"You said we were going to feel safer, Akiviak. It is the opposite."

But Akiviak replied that she had lost her faith; that was her trouble.

"Depend on the Lord. Look at the sparrow; who looks after it? The Lord!"

Thus spake Akiviak with his two empty meat cellars. He who never quite learned how to gather in larders, however much he wanted to. Instead of facing reality, he chose to avoid the point and looked instead for something else on which to focus his attention. In other words, he was looking for a method of getting rid of the symptom without curing the disease itself. Like his uncle, Elijah, who cut the patient's chest so that the pain would make him forget his headache, which was the problem in the first place.

Actually, insisted Akiviak, the trouble was that it was too far to the store. Certainly it made no sense to drag their fox skins all the way to Canada, merely to drag food equally many miles back again. Was it not about time they got a store of their own in Kaktoavik too?

He talked the trader at Cape Herschel into opening a branch of his store at Kaktoavik, and made the young halfbreed, Tigotak, the storekeeper.

To start with, a sledful of the more important articles was brought in during the winter: perfumed toilet soap, salt, sugar, tea, and some flour. All this was unloaded and stacked in Akiviak's hallway. Tigotak propped up an empty orange crate and made it into a counter, placed himself on a drum which once contained syrup, used an old soapbox for the cash and declared the store open. He was rather short of stature, this Tigotak, but agile and graceful in his movements, and exceptionally obliging and generous by nature. The business exceeded their most optimistic expectations. In less than a month the entire stock was disposed of. The only trouble was that no one except Akiviak had any money to pay for it. Thus, Akiviak ended up buying out his own store.

"You will see, everything will turn out well in the end," said Akiviak (most likely to comfort himself), and dished out the money to pay for the whole lot. He did realize, however, that he had to keep an eye on the storekeeper, who was slow at arithmetic and a little too naive to be a good businessman. When he bought a bar of soap for five cents, he sold the bar for the same price and said it was the volume of sale that made the profit.

When the supply ship came in the fall, Akiviak got hold of an empty paraffin drum which he cut in two and made into a stove and to which he attached a pipe of zinc for a smokestack. In this stove he burned a mixture of driftwood and blubber. When it was really cold he took peat, which he had dug from the marshy tundra in the summer, and dipped it in seal oil. This made the stove red hot when it burned. And the thrifty Tigotak gave him, most generously, a brand-new kerosene lamp complete with a shiny new glass, but the kerosene for the lamp naturally had to be bought from Tigotak, paid in cash. Having gotten used to this new lamp which burned with a much brighter light than the old blubber lamp, he naturally had to continue to buy kerosene as long as his money lasted. Thus he became Tigotak's most faithful customer. For only Akiviak had a regular income; he received a preacher's salary every month from the mission in the United States. The rest of the villagers were more uncertain; their income fluctuated with the game.

However, Akiviak was also quite imaginative and thrifty. He went his own way, always trying something new, but more often than not the aim of his enterprises was for the good of all. He got the idea of nailing a chunk of blubber to a pole, which he put up just outside his door. When a polar bear came for the blubber, the dogs signalled the alarm. Thus he could shoot the bear from the door. And if it happened to be a mother bear with cubs, he would shoot the mother and sell the cubs alive to a zoo in the States.

"It is a matter of making something out of what little there is," claimed Akiviak.

One winter night someone banged on Akiviak's door. Akiviak went out. A stranger, and a foreigner at that, was standing outside the door. The door was not locked, but he was not about to come in. "I am the missionary inspector. I want to talk to you," he said briskly.

"Please step inside."

"No, not here. I want to speak with you at Tigotak's. I shall wait for you there." Then he turned around and walked away.

Akiviak dressed and went to Tigotak's. There he found the inspector, a man with a ruddy complexion and a dissatisfied look on his face. He came from the States, had come all the way from

Chicago, traveling the entire coast from Point Barrow to visit all those who belonged to his faith. It had taken him over a month. And what had he found? Yes, he had found that Akiviak paid very little attention to his congregation. Now he wanted to know: why was Akiviak not out among the people doing his job?

Akiviak was paralyzed, speechless with humiliation. Here this foreigner came from far away and got him up in the middle of the night. The fact that he had passed Akiviak's house and taken in at Tigotak's was in itself an insult. And on top of it all Akiviak was scolded for not being eager enough to convert more people, for not competing more actively with the other sects for the uncommitted souls. Here stood Akiviak, astonished, fumbling for words, trying to find an explanation. Then he said quietly:

"But they do believe in our God. Even though the denomination is different, the Lord is the same."

The inspector was visibly shocked. Then he became annoyed:

"Believe, you said? Oh, no. To believe is not enough. They must believe as *we* do. And besides, the congregation must grow. Without growth, no gain. Stagnation. That which does not grow will wither away. Growth is essential. You are committed to recruit. Your congregation must expand."

All this was more than enough to take the breath away from Akiviak.

"But they all come to me for the sake of the Gospel, by their own free will. I do my best, but I cannot be everywhere at once. Only the Holy Ghost can do that."

The inspector was firm. He was not going to yield an inch:

"Your best is not good enough. I shall advise our Elders to put someone else here in your place."

"Then do that," said Akiviak.

But no one else was put in Akiviak's place.

Some time later, however, a boxful of radios arrived. They were to be distributed among the poor people of Kaktoavik. The inspector had felt pity on the unfortunate and unhappy souls up there at the uttermost end of the earth, who lived in sod houses and had none of the blessings of this world, not even a radio.

He had started raising funds among well-meaning friends in Chicago, and purchased all these radios—which no one could use in Kaktoavik because there was no electricity. And even if there was, most of them would not have been able to understand what they heard.

After the meeting with the inspector that evening, Akiviak walked along the beach on his way home. In the bright moonlight he noticed a huge log of driftwood half-buried in the sand. It occurred to him that if he could only get the log out of the sand he could use it to build a church.

The following day a storm came up from the northwest. It broke up the sea ice and the waves washed away large parts of the landbrink. When the storm was over, and it was daylight, Akiviak came out to discover that the log had been thrown on the beach just below his house. He went back in and thanked the Lord for the log. However, it was too heavy to move alone; it was at least 60 feet long. With the help of most of the able-bodied men in the village another thick log was driven under the middle of the first one. Akiviak then tied all the buckets and washtubs in the village to the free end of the log, filled them with sand, and thus tipped his log out of the sand. Then they cut it into eight equal lengths, each one measuring about seven and a half feet. In the course of the winter they split the logs with a hand saw, each log being split into seven broad boards. When spring came they built the church, measuring 15 feet by 20, covered by sod, with a wooden cross on the roof. Now Akiviak had achieved what he wanted. With his own hands he had built a house for the Lord, a meeting place for his congregation in the center of a settlement he himself had founded.

Then one day in the summer, just after the supply ship had left, Tigelok's youngest son came running into Akiviak's house with a brand-new .22 rifle in his hand.

"See what I've got!" he shouted.

Unfortunately the rifle was loaded. He must have touched the trigger. The shot went off. They heard the bang, and a thud in the wall next to the window where Sussi was sitting with her sewing.

Sussi froze. Akiviak was startled and perplexed. They heard a cry. In the confusion no one had noticed what had happened. It took some time before they had recovered from the shock, and discovered Akiviak's youngest son lying curled up on the floor in a small pool of blood. He did not complain, said nothing, just looked at them with frightened eyes. He had been hit in his stomach. He lived that day, but during the night he died. Sussi removed herself from the rest, sat alone in a corner most of the time and said nothing. She blamed no one but herself, who, like the rest of them, had taken the new inventions of the foreigners for their own gain. This was their punishment, she thought, for abandoning the ways of their forefathers. As for Akiviak, he could not forget his father who died when he ate part of a seal which had been shot with a rifle, in fact the first which came to their country.

"The Lord takes and the Lord gives. Let us be patient. You must have faith in the Lord, Sussi."

But Sussi had nothing to say.

Akiviak was unable to sleep. He would wake up fearful in the middle of the night, with a strange anxiety which somehow seemed familiar to him. It grew into a constant feeling of unrest, a fear of something he could not quite understand. Was it the vengeance of the old gods he secretly feared? What wrong had he done? Was it the new weapons, the curse which Elijah had talked about, the taboo that took his father's life? Akiviak began to look back, to remember the past. In his mind he could now see the hunters in the thickets at the Utukok River. They were seated around an oil lamp in a hunter's shelter at night, long ago. He recalled it as clearly as if it had happened only yesterday. He could see their faces now, tense, tough, weatherbeaten; he could actually smell the wet fur parkas, the odor of skins hanging to dry. He heard the hoarse voice of Elijah, in a trance, chanting, conversing with the land god Tarnavsuk, begging him to let go his curses on the young boy Apiak who was lying on the floor in a fit, about to be choked by the same evil spirits that had caused madness in their dogs. These thoughts turned in Akiviak's mind until he fell asleep and dreamt that Elijah stood over him, about to grab him by the throat and choke him. He woke to the sound of his own choking cry. Sussi had raised her head, and he heard her say:

"Why are you shouting? You frightened me."

Akiviak said he was sorry, he had had a nightmare. He stayed awake, worrying:

"Have I angered the Lord? Is this misfortune a sign of his displeasure because I have disobeyed Him? What have I done to deserve such punishment?"

He saw no reason, found no guilt. Was it then possible that the ancient gods of his forefathers were out to get him after all because he had departed from the old faith? Were the new divine powers not strong enough to protect him from the wrath of the old ones, even though he was sincere in his new faith? Or maybe the Lord was not the true God, perhaps he did not even exist at all. He started to doubt not only the existence of the Christian God, but also himself; now he was sceptical of everything. He began to fear for the future, anxious about the possible consequences of the row with the missionary inspector, who wanted to deprive him of his life's work and take away his daily bread. What would happen to him then, to his family and to his clan?

Akiviak heard Sussi sigh next to him. Then a new day dawned. They got up and went about their chores.

Relatives came to stay with them in their bereavement. Akiviak stood around, staring into open space, his face drawn. He seldom spoke. He seemed to be burdened by a nameless fear which dragged him down like an undertow. But as the days passed, something must have happened to him inside. For all of a sudden he changed completely; he became nervous, jumpy, restless and exceedingly active. During one of his prayer meetings he confessed that his sorrow had sharpened his basic Christian view of life. He felt as if he had been put to the test, as if he had come out of his inner conflict with new strength: for as he put it,

"The sorrow has blessed me with the strength of my convictions. Now I feel called upon to preach."

With renewed vigor he would now devote himself to his mission. He would work tirelessly for the salvation of his people and for the purification of his soul. He became a bundle of kinetic energy, an evangelist with all his heart and all his mind, his new battery radio bellowing on the sled. Thus he brought the Gospel from igloo to igloo on his slow journey along the coast. People could hear him coming from far away: "Here comes the Savior," they said. He went back and forth like a ball of fire, burning for his cause. Guided by conviction and desire he was constantly on the move, now here, now there. He spread the message of eternal salvation, shared his food with those who had none; gave a helping hand where needed, from sheer goodwill and faithful love for his fellow man. He did not neglect himself, however. He hunted where he could, and took a job wherever there was anything to earn. He treated himself to a recording phonograph. This he used to record songs and tales which were replayed during his prayer meetings as a source of entertainment

and attraction. Soon it was widely known that he possessed a
strange talking box that had its own spirit, that he had somebody
else's voice on rolls that could speak. People came long distances
only to see and hear if this miracle was true. Gradually people
began to gather around him; some of them even accompanied
him on his journeys. Often he arrived at the settlements with
a whole flock of followers. He was a natural leader, for he was
a man of many talents, known for his judgement and his insight.
People came to him to ask his advice before they set out on a
journey, or went out hunting. Thus he became the central figure
in a society he had helped to establish.

VIII

FOR BETTER
OR FOR WORSE

TIME passed. It changed as it always does. There were good days and there were bad days. Akiviak and Sussi had thirteen children in all. Four of them died when they were born; the rest developed, as is normally the case, depending on a combination of circumstances and inborn talents. And life followed its course: all went as it should, as seen from Akiviak's point of view.

But then the authorities, the Government, decided to introduce domesticated reindeer to the territory. The Eskimos, the killers of caribou, were to become shepherds for tame reindeer. This was decided, of course, without asking the Eskimos first. Apparently there was no reason to ask, for they hardly knew what was best for themselves. But the Government obviously did, for they were appointed to know. Otherwise, how could they exercise authority if they did not know what was good for those under their authority? Or, as Akiviak put it, "Those the Lord has selected to support us will also be granted the wisdom to do so."

The only trouble was that the Eskimos were not really suited to be the keepers of reindeer. It was like asking a goat to watch the bag of oats. Predictably, they killed the domesticated animals as long as there were reindeer left. The herds that weren't slaughtered got mixed or ran away. Then, the herdsmen could not quite agree on the pastures. This led to animosity and ill feelings. It all ended when, one night, a herd of reindeer got mixed up with a herd of caribou. In the heat of the hunt the Eskimos could hardly distinguish the one animal from the other, and killed them all.

The next thing that happened was the arrival of a couple of men, one fine day early in the summer. They came wandering along the shore carrying large packboards and round iron pans on their backs. They called themselves prospectors and asked to be taken by boat some distance up the Opelyak river. They were going to try their luck at panning for gold. They were going to get rich, build themselves a castle, fill the cellar with liquor, buy cars, and travel around the world.

Akiviak wondered how they expected to find the magic means to do all this in the desolate Opelyak River, where there was hardly a ptarmigan to be found.

Akiviak sent them along with his boys in the old wooden whaleboat. The prospectors never returned. They probably failed to find the source of their hoped-for happiness after all. But they had nevertheless managed to put some new ideas into the heads of his sons. They had suggested that the boys install an engine in the boat; then they would not have to row. His sons were persistent; in the end Akiviak exchanged the fine old whaleboat for a motor launch with a cabin and a twenty-horsepower, four-cylinder inboard engine. In addition he had to put up a lot of fox skins as well as some $400 cash to pay the difference in price between the two boats. But now he was the owner of a cruiser with a cabin the size of a house, equipped with windows to look through and benches to sit on. Now he could hold his prayer meetings there, in the cabin of the boat, as he traveled along the coast. He could see the advantage of this, naturally. He placed himself at the front of the cabin with his bible in his hand, but found that the ceiling was not high enough for him to stand upright; Whenever he straightened himself he hit his head on one of the beams. So the boys went to work. They tore off the roof, added another board to the sides, and replaced the roof.

"That is better," said Akiviak. But by now the motorboat looked like a battleship, with a tower for a cabin. Nevertheless, it was the first craft of its kind there on the coast, and its owner, Akiviak attained an added status. But it also caused him considerable concern and worry, as is the case with all shipowners. For it soon became evident that the boys had little interest in maintaining the boat. They were also rather late bringing the boat up on land in the fall, but as Akiviak said, nothing is so bad that it does not prove to be good for something. For by this time the snow covered the ground, and they could hitch their dogs to the boat and pull it like a sled. But the cooling water in the engine had frozen. In the following spring when they tried to start the engine, they discovered that the freezing had caused one of the cylinders to crack. But the boys knew what to do. They simply removed the piston, stuffed an old gunnysack into the cylinder and operated the engine all summer long on three cylinders. This worked well enough, and Akiviak, who had forgotten that the damage was caused by his sons' negligence, was proud of their ingenuity.

This was the summer when a group of foreigners who called themselves geologists found their way to Kaktoavik. They were to make a map of the country and to examine the mountains. They needed Akiviak's motorboat, and were prepared to pay $20 a day for it. This was more than he could expect to make by hunting and trapping at that time. Furthermore, he could make this money without doing anything at all for it. Naturally,

Akiviak accepted the offer. He addressed them as geologists and thanked them. They called him shipowner, shook his hand and bowed as they left. They lived in a tent by a small lake on the other side of the lagoon.

In the evening they returned, drunk. They staggered into the church in the middle of Akiviak's prayer meeting; it was Sunday. Akiviak was standing by the door reading from his bible. He asked them to be quiet. Then one of the geologists got angry and jumped on him. He was a redhaired, hot-tempered fellow. He approached Akiviak with his fist raised, called him a fool and asked him if he intended to make trouble. If so, he was going to get what he asked for, this fool of an Eskimo who took the liberty of insulting a white man. Akiviak remained calm, and looked him straight in the eye. It worked; the stranger, deflated, now quieted down. His raised arm eventually dropped, and before long he had his hands fully occupied trying to keep his balance. Then one of his pals came forward, got hold of Akiviak's shoulder and tried to pull him down. But Akiviak resisted, hanging on to the door with one hand, holding the bible with the other. Thus he stood his ground. The congregation quickly withdrew, trying to hide in the corners, scuffling for the positions closest to the wall where they were safest. Only an old widow remained in her seat. She bent forward and fixed her eyes on Akiviak. With the bible in one hand, he hung on to the door with the other. He could only think: I must stand as an example for my followers. And as he struggled he spoke to his congregation in his native tongue:

"Let us forgive them, for they know not what they do. They are not responsible for their misdeeds. The blame is on Satan who has led them into drinking. We who are saved must behave like Christians. We must stand together on the side of the Lord, and pray to Him for strength to show them the way."

Eventually the strangers gave up and left. The next day they returned sober, apologized, and gave Akiviak a bottle of liquor to smooth things over. Akiviak took the bottle, went out and smashed it against a stone in front of the visitors. Then they left. When they brought the boat back it was painted a bright red. And when Akiviak, together with Sussi, used it on a seal hunt, he noticed that the seals were frightened away. Even when he stopped the engine and rowed very quietly, the seals slipped into the water long before they got within range. This had never happened before.

"They paid you well for the boat, but you lost your hunting luck in the bargain. I think the seals see red when they see you coming," said Sussi.

Akiviak knew that Sussi was right, as usual. And because she was right, it hurt all the more.

In the wake of the geologists there came others, this time looking for oil. They were heading up the Colville River to the area around Umiat to search and to drill. Now they wanted to hire Akiviak as a guide, and his sons as handymen. But what was the point, Akiviak wanted to know. The answer was that they were going to sell the oil as fuel and make money on it. Then it dawned on Akiviak. He saw the prospect of getting gasoline for his motorboat and kerosene for his lamps, and he thought:

"Maybe we will have a pipeline from Umiat all the way down to my house. Then all I need to do is turn on the faucet and we can tank directly and don't have to go to Cape Herschel or wait for the supply ship to bring us the fuel. We will have our own supply!"

Of course he would join them. They charged across the tundra, a caravan of weasels and tractors. Soon his sons were trained drivers, leaving broad tracks in the peat as they wound their way into the mountains. Once in a while the foreigners decided to use the weasels to hunt mountain sheep. They took Akiviak as a guide, and his sons came along to help carry the meat. And so they tracked their way through the same wilderness where Akiviak as a boy had walked on foot with his bow and arrow. But when the sheep were seen feeding high up in the mountains, it was Akiviak who got there first. The boys climbed after him with their packs. The strangers came last, panting and shooting. And when they missed it was Akiviak or the boys who killed the game, so tactfully that the strangers thought that they themselves had hit the sheep. Elated with the joy of their own imagined skill, they gladly gave a bonus to the Eskimos, who merely looked at one another. They did not even shake their heads, for they had already adapted to the new situation. Then, on top of it all, they were given the meat: the hunters were only after the head.

One day on their way down from the mountains they were driving the weasel across an old glacial moraine not far from the watershed. The valley sloped to the south; to the north the landscape widened into the tundra extending all the way down to the Arctic Ocean.

"I think I recognize this place; I must have been here before," thought Akiviak. And when he discovered the remains of some birch bundles around the hillock, and the places where snares had been secured between the larger stones, he was sure. This was the place where he, as a little boy, took part in his first caribou kill. At once he could recall the vivid picture from the past. He saw his grandfather squat down behind the large block of stone, there to his left, he himself lying down behind him, shaking with excitement. He heard the thundering roar of the galloping herd of caribou storming up the valley, saw his grandfather leap from his hiding place, heard him shout, chase the herd, stab his horn dagger into the heart of the caribou in the nearest snare.

At this point the weasel thrashed through a birch bundle. Dried twigs were flying everywhere, and there, just in front of the vehicle, Akiviak saw briefly an old weather-bleached bone dagger sticking out of the gravel. A moment later the weasel had rolled over it. Akiviak turned around and saw pieces of the dagger scattered in the weasel track. He felt as if they had gone into his own heart.

"Stop!", he shouted to his son, who was at the wheel. But the weasel roared on. He shouted again, this time so as to be heard through the roar of the engine. But his son in the driver's seat merely shook his head and yelled back:

"No reason to stop here!" They drove on until they reached the camp at Umiat, where they continued to look for oil.

As the summer came to an end and ice formed on the mountain lakes during the night, the oil exploration adventure ended for that year. The drillers left with their mountain sheep trophies; Akiviak and the boys returned home with their bonus.

Then one day they had been out hunting seal. The women were busy butchering the catch. The hunters sat around watching the women, discussing the hunt. Suddenly a buzzing noise came from the distance, a humming in the air like a swarm of mosquitos on a hot summer day. Then a strange bird with stiff, motionless wings gliding down from the mountains over the tundra. It flew faster than any bird they had ever seen before. Then it landed by the lagoon, and rolled along the sand. By then, some of them had realized that this must be one of the flying machines they had heard about, a mechanical miracle that could rise in the air and fly like a bird. The Eskimos stood up, put their hands over their eyes to shield the sun, and looked at one another.

When one of the Eskimos started to run, they all followed to see what this was all about. They found a strange-looking machine on the ground with large wings and small wheels, and standing next to it a potbellied man throwing candy to the kids, who were the first to arrive on the scene. Akiviak stepped forward while the rest of the crowd remained at a distance. He greeted the man in the foreigner's tongue. The man explained that he had come to look for a suitable place for airplanes such as this one to land. He had seen from the air that the sandspit, the site of the Eskimo village, was ideal. There they could easily make a landing strip almost a mile and a half long, and at least sixty feet wide. The only trouble was the village—all the houses were in the way. They had to be moved. Why not? It would be just as nice to live on the brink overlooking the ocean. Surely they would not object to moving a little further to the west? Akiviak hesitated. It was not that simple to pull down their homes and the church. There was a harbor with shelter for their boats behind the sandspit; there were seals, fish and birds, and above all they liked it here!

All this was clear to the man who came with the airplane. He could understand it perfectly, naturally. But it would pay them to move in the long run, he explained. There would be considerable advantages. And besides, they had to keep up with the times, take part in the march of progress!

While Akiviak was considering the proposition, the pilot turned to the women. He was generous. To her utter delight Sussi was given a brand-new teapot; it had not even been taken out of its cardboard box. In addition she was presented with a set of porcelain Japanese teacups, individually wrapped in silk paper.

Afterwards the pilot persuaded Akiviak to come along for a ride. In the midst of the jubilant crowd Akiviak climbed into the plane, and was strapped to his seat next to the pilot. Then the youngsters in the crowd lifted the tail of the plane as instructed, and turned it around facing the wind. The engine was started. They were on their way. Akiviak panicked and wanted to get out, but now it was too late. The plane went faster than any dog could run. It bounced and jumped, shot up into the air, only to fall down again. The engine roared, the propeller buzzed. Then all of a sudden they were in the air, and stayed there. They climbed, circling around. Akiviak calmed down, looked around and gazed below. And there he could see everything he knew, but it all looked completely different: pack ice and ocean, coast-line, people and houses, lagoon and boats. He became very excited. The matter was settled; now he was sold. The houses had to be moved, to give room for this miracle. And the speed with which it moved! By plane one could go anywhere in no time, that he could see.

First came a single airplane, once. Then once in a while, then more often. Later on came more airplanes one after the other, sometimes two at once. They buzzed in the air, they roared on the ground. The few bewildered seals that were left popped their heads out of the sea and gazed with round incredulous eyes. Then they snorted and disappeared forever.

In the beginning Akiviak always went to meet the plane. As time passed he only appeared if there were important persons on board. In the end he did not go down to meet the plane at all. Now they had to come to him.

One fine day a huge boat came in from the sea. It came sliding in like a whole island. It resembled the ships they had seen in pictures from the war, ships which used to land the troops at Guam. The ship stopped and remained out at sea, as if it were waiting for something. Then a motor launch came shooting in against the shore. Its passengers wanted to get hold of Akiviak, who was familiar with the harbor. They needed him to pilot them in. And this he did. From the top of the bridge he took over, pointed and commanded, guiding this colossal ship with its nose towards land. As he pushed the bow of the ship up on the beach it sounded like an ice floe being grounded. Slowly a broad iron door opened in the bow, then the whole bow was opened, like the mouth of a whale, as the door dropped to the ground. Out of this huge opening came a tractor larger than a house, a bulldozer, and then ploughs and shovels mounted on all kinds of vehicles, with or without wheels.

Tents were quickly erected on the tundra. The strangers started to scrape away the earth and to even out the sand. The Eskimos who had lived there much of their lives were scurrying around trying to remove all their belongings in time. They moved into a tent camp on the landbrink for the time being. Sussi did not like it there. "We cannot live here in the winter," she said. But Akiviak scoffed at her: "We face that problem when the time comes."

As the houses were emptied, the bulldozers came thundering along and leveled them to the ground, in some cases grabbing an entire house in a single scoop.

The Eskimos were left with their hands hanging. They watched with amazement the enormous destructive powers which the foreign technology had at its disposal. They viewed the change with a mixture of fear and admiration.

At Kaktoavik there was now an enormous burst of activity. In this sudden and drastic revolution Akiviak was the hub in a wheel; everything seemed to revolve around him. He served as agent for labor, for he controlled the manpower. In addition he exercised authority and influence over the rest of his people. For this reason it was politically sound for the foreigners to have Akiviak on their side. The first thing he did was to find suitable jobs for his grownup sons Abraham, Isaac and Jacob. They were employed by the construction company responsible for the project. They were put to work tearing down what their parents had built. Next they were to level out the ground, prepare the foundation for the runway (which was to be surfaced with asphalt), unload the landing craft, transport the cargo to a temporary tent camp on the tundra some distance away, and put up the military barracks at the end of the runway. All this had to be done in a hurry, for the outside work had to be finished before freezeup. Consequently they worked in shifts around the clock. This meant that they had to sleep when the foreman told them to, according to schedule, not when they felt like it as had been their custom. However, whenever they felt the urge, felt like making a trip somewhere or to go hunting, well, they just took off. This they were used to, for they were a migratory people. And this the construction company had to accept; it was of no use to argue. Nor did it help to scold them or to bark at them. For the Eskimos merely grinned, without really understanding what the fuss was all about.

However, these Eskimos had a great deal of technical talent, and they learned very quickly. It was not long before they were driving both tractors and trucks just as well as anybody else. And now they were sitting at the controls, in the driver's seat, wiping out their own foundations, and the houses which their parents had so laboriously built upon them. Like all young people, they liked speed, and charged ahead. They also had a knack for mechanical things, such as engines, and quickly learned how they worked. They were masters at improvisation; they could repair and fix almost anything. And here they saw an opportunity to make money, fast and easy. But the money went out as fast as it came in; it was spent on all kinds of useless gadgets. As long as it was something new they would buy it. Akiviak, however, was different. He sent his income by registered mail to Fairbanks, where he had it put in an account and recorded in a bank book. He had finally turned capitalist. He even had money to lend; he charged interest and served as some kind of a bank. He signed for the wages on behalf of the working Eskimos and distributed the money, and no one could complain as long as they depended on him. He financed the store; Tigotak had to accept the fact that he was merely the manager. And when Sussi sighed and felt that she had lost control of things, Akiviak would say to her: "You should wish that events may go the way they are going, for then they are going your way."

With construction in full swing, the Eskimos had their hands full getting out of the way of the forces of destruction. They were running back and forth carrying their most precious articles from their homes. But much was lost; this could not be avoided, said Akiviak. Every time the bulldozer took a break, the Eskimos were there to dig for their belongings.

Even Sussi was poking in the ruins. When Akiviak saw this he asked what she was looking for. Sussi answered, without looking up: "My charm, the amulet you gave me the year we were married." Akiviak wanted to comfort her, for he was in a generous mood: "Never mind, I will give you some earrings made of glass, with a hook to hang on your ears instead, the kind I showed you in the mail order catalog." But Sussi preferred her old amulet nevertheless. It had a certain value to her, for purely sentimental reasons. More was not said about the matter, for now the bulldozer was on its way and Akiviak could only pull Sussi out of its reach.

Their son Isaac was driving the bulldozer. Akiviak was proud of his son, even though he was tearing down what Akiviak himself had taken so long to build.

In this drastic transition Akiviak was the middleman, standing with one leg in the old, the other in the new era.

It happened that some of the older men came to Akiviak to express a certain apprehension, an uncertainty about all these new enterprises, a fear of revenge from the spirits. And even though he reassured them, and said that this was progress, they had planted a seed of doubt in Akiviak's mind as well. Especially old Paneak. Paneak carried a certain weight with Akiviak, for he always spoke on the basis of experience. He could remind Akiviak of certain events from their mutual past; of occasions when someone broke a taboo, and what had happened in consequence. This kindled Akiviak's doubt, aroused the old fear, a strange apprehension which emerged when it was dark and when he was half asleep. One night he dreamt that his own name-soul, his great grandfather Akiviak, came to him in the twilight, shaking his head, looking at him accusingly. Then the spirit vanished. In its place Akiviak now saw the Kivitok midget, the one he had seen riding on a caribou in a dream long ago. This time the midget sat on the seat of a tractor and laughed in a most peculiar way, as if he was enjoying someone else's misfortune.

Akiviak woke up. The construction manager was standing in the doorway, asking him to get up. He needed help to unload a ship that had just arrived with some cargo.

By now things were really jumping in Kaktoavik. Construction workers were running in all directions, boxes, crates, materials and machines were everywhere. The foreigners were looking for souvenirs of any kind. There was hardly a thing the Eskimos would not sell and turn into money, anything from old, useless harpoons to new skin boats. And the foreigners were willing to pay the price. They were quite generous in this respect. Akiviak was alert enough to see the opportunity, and smart enough to grasp it for the benefit of his clan. He put Sussi to work sewing mukluks. But she was too meticulous, sewing every stitch with the same care as she did when she made mukluks for herself or her family. Akiviak was impatient; he thought she was too compulsive. He was thinking of the profit. They had to utilize the opportunity now while the foreigners were there, while there was a market for their products, while the demand was at its greatest.

"Oh, you are too fussy," he reproached Sussi. "Use longer stitches; there is no need to make such tight seams. The mukluks are merely going for looks, not for wear."

But Sussi could not be different, for such was her nature. She had only one standard: her own. As far as she was concerned, a stitch was a stitch. But Akiviak was as inventive as his wife was accurate. He put all the other women to work as well, sewing parkas, mittens and all kinds of fancy products. This soon developed into a flourishing home industry.

Akiviak was again the middleman; all the buying and all the selling that went on, every transaction, went through him. He knew what the prices were in Fairbanks—no one could fool him. And he let nothing, and no one, go to waste. An Eskimo boy with a severe physical handicap (he was missing most of his fingertips), who could therefore not be employed as a construction worker, was put to work carving figures in bone. A child who could hardly write was encouraged to draw pictures of daily life. Akiviak sent his own daughter to wash dishes in the construction camp. There was a market for everything; the more primitive, the better. Soon they hardly knew what to do with their money. For by now everybody had radios, cameras, phonographs, and more chewing gum than they could use. And the kids had more candy than was good for them.

Akiviak was still the boat-owner, no, shipowner, and had developed quite a charter business. He rented out his motor launch, not merely to transport supplies and cargo here and there, but also for sightseeing, for guided tours among the pack ice, for hunting expeditions looking for seals, caribou, fox, lemming, and ground squirrels. The foreigners thought it well worth the money. And if they were so fortunate as to kill anything, they gladly gave Akiviak a bonus. In any case he got the meat, for the only thing that interested the foreigners was the skin and the head. And Akiviak availed himself of every opportunity to make a plug for his store. He ordered a little of almost everything from the mail order catalog and had the goods shipped to him, free of charge, by plane from Fairbanks. They sold like hotcakes, even though some of the stuff was produced in Japan and could be purchased cheaper at home, and most of it was useless. But to the foreigners, a trinket from Akiviak's store was a souvenir to take home as a reminder of tough times by the shores of the Polar Sea. Besides, on what else could they spend their money at Kaktoavik?

Akivak rubbed his hands and said to Sussi:

"Now everything is going our way!"

"It is going the way it is," said Sussi.

In the evening Akiviak arranged a drum dance for the foreigners and sold tickets at the door. This turned out to be a most popular affair. It filled the house several evenings running. And Akiviak took the opportunity to finish off with a sermon and a prayer meeting. Thus he secured full attendance for his prayer meeting as well. And it impressed the rest of the Eskimos in the village that the foreigners also came to Akiviak to hear the Gospel.

But when the construction had progressed to the point that the barracks, including the dining room and the recreation room were finished, and the foreigners started to show cowboy films in the evenings, Akiviak got stiff competition. Many of the Eskimos preferred to see violence rather than read the Bible. This Akiviak was prepared to tolerate as long as it only took place on the weekdays. But when some of the younger Eskimos also started going to the movies on Sunday evenings, he put his foot down: now they had gone too far. This he could not tolerate. Not that he was against the movies; in fact he himself attended them at times. One evening they ran the film about King Solomon's mines, in which the negroes from Africa were beating their drums and dancing barefooted. The Eskimos immediately identified themselves with the dancers. It appeared as if their own ancient souls were speaking to them through a drum language which they recognized: a rhythm which still was embedded in their bodies, dormant urges which now were called to life. It brought out memories in the old people, it stimulated the younger ones. In the end they were all stepping in time to the beat; they jumped up in ecstasy, yelled with the dancers, rejoiced when the spears flew and the dance went around the offering fire. At that moment they had returned to their origin, to that most ancient time; they were their own selves again, the way they had been originally. And so they sang all through the late summer night.

IX

AT THE END
OF THE TRAIL

LIFE went on as usual in the village.

Akiviak fussed around and busied himself with his many projects and the running of the community. He became a nervous wreck from all the stress, and developed a persistent headache from all the problems he created for himself. In the end he had to go to see a doctor in Fairbanks. He landed on the huge military airstrip outside the city, taxied up to the hangar, saw a whole fleet of multiengined aircraft lined up in a row. There were crowds of people, crowds everywhere. They were all in a hurry and few of them looked pleased. Inside, in a room as large as a cathedral, he was allowed to talk to the missionary on a telephone, a talking gadget through which he could hear the voice of a stranger. At first he thought it was the Holy Ghost he could hear in the instrument, for who else could be heard without being seen? Finally they came to collect him with a car. En route to the city they passed a pig farm, where he saw round sausages of living blubber that moved about on legs and grunted with well-being. Here was an animal according to his taste! Then he was taken to a cafè, where they had to pay for the food. This was new to him, for it had never happened among the Eskimos that one who was hungry could not freely satisfy his hunger as long as there was food available. Then he came to the clinic. There he had an X-ray taken of his skull, but nothing was found. But Akiviak kept staring at the X-ray, speechless. A miracle that they could take a picture of his insides! There was a remarkable resemblance between this X-ray and the picture he had seen of himself in the mirrorlike ice of a mountain lake many years ago.

The doctors concluded that his trouble, the headache, was most probably related to an accident he had suffered as a child, when he was hunting mountain sheep and fell off a precipice. On that basis, he was told, he could apply for a disability pension. But this was an insult. He, disabled! He who was always ahead of everyone else, always up front, the leader, the number one man, a man in the prime of his life! His only trouble was a little headache. Otherwise he was perfectly able.

"Oh, well," said the doctor, and sent him home. But then bad luck would have it that Kaktoavik was closed in by dense fog, so the plane was unable to land. They had to continue to Point Barrow instead. There they left Akiviak. Two months later they remembered their passenger, and finally came to collect him. He was taken back to Fairbanks, then north to Kaktoavik. But as the plane came in for a landing, a gust of cross-wind blew the small single-engine aircraft sideways off the landing strip. The tail-wheel touched a gasoline drum. The pilot lost control, the plane came roaring across the niggerheads, bounced over a ditch, plowed through an old whaleboat which went flying in all directions, and came diving in between the struts of a radio-antenna mast, with the result that both wings were torn off. When they finally came to a halt in front of the cabin where Sussi was waiting, there was hardly anything left of the plane but the seats.

Akiviak simply loosened the safety belt and stepped out, looked around among the spectators, and said: "There, you see, it is safe to fly!"

But Sussi, who had been waiting for several months, said that one had to have plenty of time if one were to get anywhere with an airplane! Akiviak had to admit that it would have been quicker for him to come from Point Barrow by dog team.

During Akiviak's absence they had completed the rebuilding of the village up on the brink. But the new village was by no means as good as the old one. Akiviak was dissatisfied with it all, and very critical. True enough, it had to be admitted that they had been pressed for time. They had to get the houses built before winter. They had nothing but old material, used wooden packing cases, odds and ends of all kinds. The result was, accordingly, a patched-up improvisation. They had put it all together as best they could, mended the leaking roofs and covered up the drafty cracks. And this was where he found Sussi sitting with her memories, sighing sadly, with both feet firmly planted on the earth floor. Akiviak had come with his dream about better days to come, his philosophy that in the end all will be for the best. What had become of them?

Well, the only trouble, as Akiviak saw it, was simply the fact that they had not had time to rebuild the church. That was the only thing they lacked, a house in which to praise the Lord. Akiviak went to work, gathered what was left of the old church, collected bits of new building material here and there, and built a mixture of mission and schoolhouse wall-to-wall with his own cabin. He got hold of an old generator and made an electrical plant. Now they were going to have a school for the kids so that they too might learn the language of the foreigners, like ordinary people. And the teacher came late in the summer. He was pale and said very little. But he did live there, at any rate, slept in the barracks, took his meals in the military camp and held classes occasionally. Eventually he grew a beard and became even less talkative.

The prosperity lasted a while. Then one day the good life was over. The military base was completed, the barracks were built. The camp was manned by people from the outside; the foreigners needed no further help. And for some reason, the people at the base kept to themselves, and stayed in their camp. Contact with the Eskimos was minimal; at times there was no contact at all. In any case, this relationship varied according to the attitude of the base commander.

Now came a period of recession, then depression. This hit the Eskimos harder now that they had become accustomed to a higher standard of living, an abundance of material things, and a certain level of comfort. They had never learned how to save or how to handle money, for saving was not a part of their nature. Except for Akiviak. He still had money in the bank; he was in the black and had nothing to fear. The rest had spent their money as fast as they had earned it. Now some of them felt entitled to live on Akiviak's savings, for why should he, who had saved, have more than they, who had been good about keeping the money in circulation? At any rate they could not possibly live on the cameras they had bought when the going was good. Not even the electric washing-machine, idle and rusting on the tundra between the shacks, could they use for they had neither electricity nor running water. However, they did keep it, if for no other reason than to show that they could afford to own a modern washing machine; it was a status symbol. They heated water on a stove made of an old gasoline drum, carried the hot water in buckets and poured it into the washing machine. Now no one could say that they did not follow the trend of modern times.

Once more fox traps were set; there was no getting around it. But this time they used traps of iron instead of wood. The new ones had to be purchased and they were expensive. They were also more difficult to use than the old ones, required more care, had to be inspected more frequently, and failed more often. But there were not many foxes around, and the few they did trap were scruffy, with a pelt of little value. In addition the price of the skin was low. But there was an abundance of wolf, and the bounty had increased to $60 apiece. The reason was that the authorities believed it was the wolf that had diminished the caribou herds. So the Eskimos at Kaktoavik started to hunt wolf. And for a long time the bounty was all they lived on, excepting some ptarmigan and ground squirrels, and an odd seal now and then. Now all was well until the authorities launched their drive to exterminate the wolves. They wiped them out with shotguns fired from low-flying aircraft out on the tundra.

Thus even the wolves became extinct. But the ones that suffered most from this were the caribou. They developed a hoof disease, a kind of fungus infection. Because the caribou were now left unmolested by the wolf and could remain feeding and stepping about in the same place for long periods at a time, the infection soon spread to the entire herd. Sussi soon realized the implications of what had happened. She said. "One should not fool around with nature."

Akiviak was more flexible by nature, and consoled himself with the fact that a wolf is a wolf; in any case it is a bad egg.

"But what are we going to live on, then?" asked Sussi. Could he tell her?

"There will always be a way," insisted Akiviak.

And, strangely enough, he proved to be right. By sheer luck the authorities, this remarkable institution operating somewhere south of the mountains, had decided to introduce a new kind of award which could only be granted to unmarried mothers. They were given $60 a month for each child they bore without being legally married. Kaktoavik was blessed with the good fortune of having one such person, Linda, the mother of three. She received $180 each month, almost equivalent to a catch of one wolf per week. And this was good hunting, enough to feed almost the entire village. Thus, this young unmarried mother became a provider, a benefactor, almost a goddess. She was looked upon as a sacred person who could not be allowed to marry, even if she wanted to. They simply could not afford it, no matter what Akiviak had to say about it, and however great a sin it was. Besides, no one needed to spend money on ammunition to keep Linda pregnant. And as for Linda, this situation seemed to suit her, for she had always been a bit flighty and cared little for the idea of having to stick to one man only. And as long as she moved about and looked large around the middle all those who lived on her income felt safe and secure. Every time she gave birth the contribution increased, and the money poured in. However, she did know how to take advantage of her status. She had the upper hand, and she used her power. No one had anything to say when there was something she really wanted. Her power exceeded even that of Akiviak, who for his part had a keen appreciation of the situation. He felt that one had to accept the facts of life, had to use common sense:

"Nothing is so bad that it is not good for something." And in this again he proved to be right. When all things appeared at their darkest—a year had passed without any babies from Linda—something unexpected happened. A man arrived by plane one day. He wore a fur coat, carried a large black briefcase under his arm, and said he represented the welfare department. Akiviak blessed him. The visitor assured them that he came for the sole purpose of finding out who among the Eskimos at Kaktoavik was eligible for unemployment compensation. Unemployment compensation? What was that, Akiviak wanted to know. Well, this was a form of social security, a grant from the Government to all those who were out of work, a social benefit considered and approved by the Congress. It was now merely a question as to who in Kaktoavik was out of work, who was unemployed in the technical sense of the law. Work? No one worked in Kaktoavik, Akiviak assured him without hesitation. He knew, of course, but judged it unnecessary to say that for an Eskimo hunting, trapping, and fishing are not considered work, merely fun. Therefore, everyone was indeed out of work. Thus Akiviak reasoned with himself.

The official took a pause, looked around and said: "Well, you are all unemployed here, then?"

This Akiviak could verify with good conscience.

"I understand," said the official. But the law stated that they must have been employed three months out of the year, and then become unemployed in order to qualify for compensation. But this they had done! They had been employed in the building of the base had been on the payroll all summer long! The official brightened. He said: "There you are!" And the official recorded in his ledger the names of all able-bodied men in the village. The exact date of birth they could not give him, unfortunately, for they had not, so far, had any use for it and consequently they had not kept records. But they guessed by mutual effort as best they could, and arrived at something reasonable for each individual, and added this to the official's list for completeness' sake. And this was how it happened that the entire village, more or less, with the exception of Akiviak who was a salaried preacher received social benefit unemployment compensation. Never before had they been more secure. But not until the official had left did Akiviak himself feel quite safe. Then he said to Sussi:

"Was this not what I told you, Sussi? Surely the Lord looks after his flock."

But Sussi didn't smile as she looked at him. Her face was a yellowish hue. She had complained about pains in her stomach, and her skin was itching all over, driving her crazy. She could not tolerate her food, especially the blubber. And her stools were light-colored, almost white, like the flour balls they used in the meat soup. Finally she got so sick that Akiviak had to ask the military commander at the camp for help. Sussi and Akiviak were flown to Fairbanks by military plane. Sussi was taken to see the doctor. He said she suffered from gallstones, and that it was a fairly common complaint for a woman of her age; the best thing to do would be to wait and see. Then he sent her home as yellow as she was when she arrived. She became worse as the weeks passed. And when she reappeared in Fairbanks she was admitted to the hospital at once. They operated on her right away, and found that she had cancer of the liver. She had waited too long, they said. Nothing could help her now. All they could do was close her up and wait for the end. Akiviak was so shocked that he became quite ill.

He was living in the basement of the church, and came to see Sussi in the morning and in the evening. He was coughing constantly. One day when his coughing was especially bad he noticed a bulging tumor in his groin. It did not hurt very much, and he managed to press the lump back in with his fingers. But then, after a violent sneeze the tumor reappeared. Now it was really painful, and this time he was unable to push it back in place. "Hernia," said the physician. After the operation Akiviak was placed in the room next to Sussi's. Through the thin wall he could hear her moans.

One day Sussi died. "In her sleep," said the nurse, in order to comfort Akiviak. He had barely enough strength to follow her to the chapel. He walked, bent as a cripple, behind the coffin the weary path from the church to the chapel. Sussi herself had asked to be buried among her kinsfolk at home. Now they flew the body to Kaktoavik and buried it on the brink of the Polar Sea.

Akiviak returned to Kaktoavik in the spring. The snow was melting. Water was dripping from the roof, there was sunshine on the ice. The snow bunting whistled faintly on the southern slopes. Akiviak felt lonely at home. He looked at his bed and thought it was too broad for him alone. But time passed, as it always does. And when a year had gone by he again was grateful that spring had come. He felt that he was still strong, and sensed an almost painful feeling of manhood below his belt. He looked around and his eyes fell upon the young Sara, who was single, well-developed, and friendly with the trader Tigotak. Akiviak spoke to her in private, presented his desire and his bankbook.

She was no fool. She saw the advantages. The only trouble was, she saw the disadvantages as well. She hesitated, oscillating between Akiviak and Tigotak—one with the money and the prestige, the other with the young, strong body. In the end it was the money that settled the issue. Akiviak was to be wed again, to Sara. He sent her home that evening with her arms full of canned food. He gathered the entire village in his house for a drum dance in the living room, to eat, sing, and dance. Then Akiviak sang gently to start with, then with vigor and force. The drummers egged him on, whipped up his spirit. Akiviak had not felt so young in many years as in that dance. Once again he was his old self.

Now he was again the singer, the actor who made up his verses and sang them as he danced.

He let himself go. In his strange mood, blurred by the trance of the drumbeat, he worked himself into sheer ecstasy, possessed by the strange feelings of the past, spurred by sleeping desires and ancient instincts that were now awakened anew.

Once more he is the man from a stone age as he dances in the dimly lit room; he sees in a glance the picture of Holy Mary on the wall. Was it Sussi? or perhaps Sara? He merely senses the resemblance, he no longer can distinguish one from the other, as in his trance they blend together, become one. Now the pictures return, pictures from a past that before had been too distant to recall, memories of a night in a skin tent in a blizzard on the tundra. He hears the whirling snow, the vibrations in the tent under the pressure of the wind. The drums are throbbing. This sound is transformed into the hiss of blowing snow sweeping across the smoke-tanned caribou skins of the tent. Akiviak swirls on in his rhythmic dance. As if it were a whisper from far away he now can hear the gale; he can hear its voice, whispering, roaring. He sees the white expanse of the wilderness, the flickering light of a blizzard in the night; white herds of riding statues, driven by the storm. He listens to the wind, the night is suddenly bright around him. He listens, and the wind speaks to him in a whisper, as he lies snugly in the skins waiting for the dawn. The voice says to him: "Never mind the wind, sleep in peace, dull your hunger." His eyes scan the wall as he swirls around in his dance. There he sees weapons of recent years, a radio, some rubbish, the gleaming light of an electric bulb swaying from the ceiling. His mood changes, his sense of time reverses, now he sees the future, a church full of light and crystal, an altar, his own wedding with Sara. In the candlelight below the cross above the altar, there is a world of joy.

All this he sang about as he danced, and then at the end the song was a cry.

The drums ceased, silence fell upon the dancers and the crowd.

Akiviak flew to Fairbanks with Sara, went to the minister to be wed. The minister asked for their health certificates. They had none and went to the doctor. He discovered that Sara had tuberculosis. Thus they were unable to get married after all, for the law did not permit people with active tuberculosis to get married, obviously to prevent the disease from spreading.

Thus, they returned to Kaktoavik unmarried, Akiviak with a mixture of bitterness and guilt. For he believed that tuberculosis was the disease of the foreigners, a plague from the south. This was their punishment for having given up their own heritage, their integrity, their culture, sacrificing the freedom of their forefathers for the ways of the foreigners. "Our body is the same, exactly as before," he wondered. "Is it possible that our soul has changed?"

He never completely attained peace of mind. Doubt haunted him, and a dark mood came over him at night. He used to lie awake, filled with fear. Then he viewed everything in the dimmest of lights, saw all his shortcomings, his wrongdoings, his misdeeds, doubted everything, all his life's work, only to view it all in a brighter light at dawn. But now his smile was gone; his laughter and his will to live had left him.

He ended his life as he had begun, the hunter in pursuit of the game. It was a December day. Akiviak was out on the ice, hunting bearded seal together with the trader Tigotak. Afterwards Tigotak had this to say: "Akiviak had just harpooned an ugruk in a breathing hole on the ice, was holding it with the harpoon line in one hand, trying to remove his rifle from the sled with the other hand to kill the seal. He grabbed the rifle by the barrel and tried to loosen it from the sled. Suddenly the seal jerked, and Akiviak pulled on the rifle. The trigger caught in some gear on the sled, the shot went off, and the bullet hit him in the head."

But those who examined Akiviak's rifle afterwards said that they could see no gunsmoke in the nozzle. And the bullet had entered his skull from the back.

They buried him, his head facing North, with the harpoon in his right hand, the rifle in his left, the man who carried the weapons of the stone age and the atomic age. But the man had remained the same. Only the times had changed.

The aurora glowed like a torch under the North Star. This too had been the same always. It had flowed over him when, as a boy, he kneeled on the ice and saw the universe reflected in his own mirror image; when he kindled the fire with his flint and trailed the caribou across the tundra. And it flowed over him now, lifeless in his grave. It came and it went as it had always done, under the North Star.

And the wind swept the snow across the crust and wiped out the tracks he had left.

There is nothing more to say, for Akiviak was no more.